**E.W Hornung**

# The Thousandth Woman

E.W Hornung

# The Thousandth Woman

1st Edition | ISBN: 978-3-75238-360-7

Place of Publication: Frankfurt am Main, Germany

Year of Publication: 2020

Outlook Verlag GmbH, Germany.

# THE
# THOUSANDTH WOMAN

## By
## ERNEST W. HORNUNG

# I
# A SMALL WORLD

Cazalet sat up so suddenly that his head hit the woodwork over the upper berth. His own voice still rang in his startled ears. He wondered how much he had said, and how far it could have carried above the throb of the liner's screws and the mighty pounding of the water against her plates. Then his assembling senses coupled the light in the cabin with his own clear recollection of having switched it off before turning over. And then he remembered how he had been left behind at Naples, and rejoined the *Kaiser Fritz* at Genoa, only to find that he no longer had a cabin to himself.

A sniff assured Cazalet that he was neither alone at the moment nor yet the only one awake; he pulled back the swaying curtain, which he had taken to keeping drawn at night; and there on the settee, with the thinnest of cigarettes between his muscular fingers, sat a man with a strong blue chin and the quizzical solemnity of an animated sphinx.

It was his cabin companion, an American named Hilton Toye, and Cazalet addressed him with nervous familiarity.

"I say! Have I been talking in my sleep?"

"Why, yes!" replied Hilton Toye, and broke into a smile that made a human being of him.

Cazalet forced a responsive grin, as he reached for his own cigarettes. "What did I say?" he asked, with an amused curiosity at variance with his shaking hand and shining forehead.

Toye took him in from crown to fingertips, with something deep behind his kindly smile. "I judge," said he, "you were dreaming of some drama you've been seeing ashore, Mr. Cazalet."

"Dreaming!" said Cazalet, wiping his face. "It was a nightmare! I must have turned in too soon after dinner. But I should like to know what I said."

"I can tell you word for word. You said, 'Henry Craven—dead!' and then you said, 'Dead—dead—Henry Craven!' as if you'd got to have it both ways to make sure."

"It's true," said Cazalet, shuddering. "I saw him lying dead, in my dream."

Hilton Toye took a gold watch from his waistcoat pocket. "Thirteen minutes to one in the morning," he said, "and now it's September eighteenth. Take a note of that, Mr. Cazalet. It may be another case of second sight for your psychical research society."

"I don't care if it is." Cazalet was smoking furiously.

"Meaning it was no great friend you dreamed was dead?"

"No friend at all, dead or alive!"

"I'm kind of wondering," said Toye, winding his watch up slowly, "if he's by way of being a friend of mine. I know a Henry Craven over in England. Lives along the river, down Kingston way, in a big house."

"Called Uplands?"

"Yes, sir! That's the man. Little world, isn't it?"

The man in the upper berth had to hold on as his curtains swung clear; the man tilted back on the settee, all attention all the time, was more than ever an effective foil to him. Without the kindly smile that went as quickly as it came, Hilton Toye was somber, subtle and demure. Cazalet, on the other hand, was of sanguine complexion and impetuous looks. He was tanned a rich bronze about the middle of the face, but it broke off across his forehead like the coloring of a meerschaum pipe. Both men were in their early prime, and each stood roughly for his race and type: the traveled American who knows the world, and the elemental Britisher who has made some one loose end of it his own.

"I thought of my Henry Craven," continued Toye, "as soon as ever you came out with yours. But it seemed a kind of ordinary name. I might have known it was the same if I'd recollected the name of his firm. Isn't it Craven & Cazalet, the stockbrokers, down in Tokenhouse Yard?"

"That's it," said Cazalet bitterly. "But there have been none of us in it since my father died ten years ago."

"But you're Henry Craven's old partner's son?"

"I'm his only son."

"Then no wonder you dream about Henry Craven," cried Toye, "and no wonder it wouldn't break your heart if your dream came true."

"It wouldn't," said Cazalet through his teeth. "He wasn't a white man to me or mine—whatever you may have found him."

"Oh! I don't claim to like him a lot," said Toye.

"But you seem to know a good deal about him?"

"I had a little place near his one summer. I know only what I heard down there."

"What did you hear?" asked Cazalet. "I've been away ten years, ever since the crash that ruined everybody but the man at the bottom of the whole thing. It would be a kindness to tell me what you heard."

"Well, I guess you've said it yourself right now. That man seems to have beggared everybody all around except himself; that's how I make it out," said Hilton Toye.

"He did worse," said Cazalet through his teeth. "He killed my poor father; he banished me to the wilds of Australia; and he sent a better man than himself to prison for fourteen years!"

Toye opened his dark eyes for once. "Is that so? No. I never heard that," said he.

"You hear it now. He did all that, indirectly, and I don't care who hears me say so. I didn't realize it at the time. I was too young, and the whole thing laid me out too flat; but I know it now, and I've known it long enough. It was worse than a crash. It was a scandal. That was what finished us off, all but Henry Craven! There'd been a gigantic swindle—special investments recommended by the firm, bogus certificates and all the rest of it. We were all to blame, of course. My poor father ought never to have been a business man at all; he should have been a poet. Even I—I was only a youngster in the office, but I ought to have known what was going on. But Henry Craven *did* know. He was in it up to the neck, though a fellow called Scruton did the actual job. Scruton got fourteen years—and Craven got our old house on the river!"

"And feathered it pretty well!" said Toye, nodding. "Yes, I did hear that. And I can tell you they don't think any better of him, in the neighborhood, for going to live right there. But how did he stop the other man's mouth, and— how do you know?"

"Never mind how I know," said Cazalet. "Scruton was a friend of mine, though an older man; he was good to me, though he was a wrong 'un himself. He paid for it—paid for two—that I *can* say! But he was engaged to Ethel Craven at the time, was going to be taken into partnership on their marriage, and you can put two and two together for yourself."

"Did she wait for him?"

"About as long as you'd expect of the breed! She was her father's daughter. I wonder you didn't come across her and her husband!"

"I didn't see so much of the Craven crowd," replied Hilton Toye. "I wasn't stuck on them either. Say, Cazalet, I wouldn't be that old man when Scruton comes out, would you?"

But Cazalet showed that he could hold his tongue when he liked, and his grim look was not so legible as some that had come and gone before. This one stuck until Toye produced a big flask from his grip, and the talk shifted to less painful ground. It was the last night in the Bay of Biscay, and Cazalet told how he had been in it a fortnight on his way out by sailing-vessel. He even told it with considerable humor, and hit off sundry passengers of ten years ago as though they had been aboard the German boat that night; for he had gifts of anecdote and verbal portraiture, and in their unpremeditated cups Toye drew him out about the bush until the shadows passed for minutes from the red-brick face with the white-brick forehead.

"I remember thinking I would dig for gold," said Cazalet. "That's all I knew about Australia; that and bushrangers and dust-storms and bush-fires! But you can have adventures of sorts if you go far enough up-country for 'em; it still pays you to know how to use your fists out there. I didn't, but I was picking it up before I'd been out three months, and in six I was as ready as anybody to take off my coat. I remember once at a bush shanty they dished up such fruity chops that I said I'd fight the cook if they'd send *him* up; and I'm blowed if it wasn't a fellow I'd been at school with and worshiped as no end of a swell at games! Potts his name was, old Venus Potts, the best looking chap in the school among other things; and there he was, cooking carrion at twenty-five bob a week! Instead of fighting we joined forces, got a burr-cutting job on a good station, then a better one over shearing, and after that I wormed my way in as bookkeeper, and my pal became one of the head overseers. Now we're our own bosses with a share in the show, and the owner comes up only once a year to see how things are looking."

"I hope he had a daughter," said Toye, "and that you're going to marry her, if you haven't yet?"

Cazalet laughed, but the shadow had returned. "No. I left that to my pal," he said. "*He* did that all right!"

"Then I advise you to go and do likewise," rejoined his new friend with a geniality impossible to take amiss. "I shouldn't wonder, now, if there's some girl you left behind you."

Cazalet shook his head. "None who would look on herself in that light," he interrupted. It was all he said, but once more Toye was regarding him as shrewdly as when the night was younger, and the littleness of the world had not yet made them confidant and boon companion.

Eight bells actually struck before their great talk ended and Cazalet swore that

5

he missed the "watches aft, sir!" of the sailing-vessel ten years before; and recalled how they had never changed watch without putting the ship about, his last time in the bay.

"Say!" exclaimed Hilton Toye, knitting his brows over some nebulous recollection of his own. "I seem to have heard of you and some of your yarns before. Didn't you spend nights in a log-hut miles and miles from any other human being?"

It was as they were turning in at last, but the question spoiled a yawn for Cazalet.

"Sometimes, at one of our out-stations," said he, looking puzzled.

"I've seen your photograph," said Toye, regarding him with a more critical stare. "But it was with a beard."

"I had it off when I was ashore the other day," said Cazalet. "I always meant to, before the end of the voyage."

"I see. It was a Miss Macnair showed me that photograph—Miss Blanche Macnair lives in a little house down there near your old home. I judge hers is another old home that's been broken up since your day."

"They've all got married," said Cazalet.

"Except Miss Blanche. You write to her some, Mr. Cazalet?"

"Once a year—regularly. It was a promise. We were kids together," he explained, as he climbed back into the upper berth.

"Guess you were a lucky kid," said the voice below. "She's one in a thousand, Miss Blanche Macnair!"

———————

6

# II
# SECOND SIGHT

Southampton Water was an ornamental lake dotted with fairy lamps. The stars above seemed only a far-away reflex of those below; but in their turn they shimmered on the sleek silken arm of sleeping sea. It was a midsummer night, lagging a whole season behind its fellows. But already it was so late that the English passengers on the *Kaiser Fritz* had abandoned all thought of catching the last train up to London.

They tramped the deck in their noisy, shiny, shore-going boots; they manned the rail in lazy inarticulate appreciation of the nocturne in blue stippled with green and red and countless yellow lights. Some delivered themselves of the patriotic platitudes which become the homing tourist who has seen no foreign land to touch his own. But one who had seen more than sights and cities, one who had been ten years buried in the bush, one with such yarns to spin behind those outpost lights of England, was not even on deck to hail them back into his ken. Achilles in his tent was no more conspicuous absentee than Cazalet in his cabin as the *Kaiser Fritz* steamed sedately up Southampton Water.

He had finished packing; the stateroom floor was impassable with the baggage that Cazalet had wanted on the five-weeks' voyage. There was scarcely room to sit down, but in what there was sat Cazalet like a soul in torment. All the vultures of the night before, of his dreadful dream, and of the poignant reminiscences to which his dream had led, might have been gnawing at his vitals as he sat there waiting to set foot once more in the land from which a bitter blow had driven him.

Yet the bitterness might have been allayed by the consciousness that he, at any rate, had turned it to account. It had been, indeed, the making of him; thanks to that stern incentive, even some of the sweets of a deserved success were already his. But there was no hint of complacency in Cazalet's clouded face and heavy attitude. He looked as if he had not slept, after all, since his nightmare; almost as if he could not trust himself to sleep again. His face was pale, even in that torrid zone between the latitudes protected in the bush by beard and wide-awake. And he jumped to his feet as suddenly as the screw stopped for the first time; but that might have been just the curious shock which its cessation always causes after days at sea. Only the same thing happened again and yet again, as often as ever the engines paused before the end. Cazalet would spring up and watch his stateroom door with clenched fists and haunted eyes. But it was some long time before the door flew open,

7

and then slammed behind Hilton Toye.

Toye was in a state of excitement even more abnormal than Cazalet's nervous despondency, which indeed it prevented him from observing. It was instantaneously clear that Toye was astounded, thrilled, almost triumphant, but as yet just drawing the line at that. A newspaper fluttered in his hand.

"Second sight?" he ejaculated, as though it were the night before and Cazalet still shaken by his dream. "I guess you've got it in full measure, pressed down and running over, Mr. Cazalet!"

It was a sorry sample of his talk. Hilton Toye did not usually mix the ready metaphors that nevertheless had to satisfy an inner censor, of some austerity, before they were allowed to leave those deliberate lips. As a rule there was dignity in that deliberation; it never for a moment, or for any ordinary moment, suggested want of confidence, for example. It could even dignify some outworn modes of transatlantic speech which still preserved a perpetual freshness in the mouth of Hilton Toye. Yet now, in his strange excitement, word and tone alike were on the level of the stage American's. It was not less than extraordinary.

"You don't mean about—" Cazalet seemed to be swallowing.

"I do, sir!" cried Hilton Toye.

"—about Henry Craven?"

"Sure."

"Has—something or other—happened to him?"

"Yep."

"You don't mean to say he's—dead?"

"Last Wednesday night!" Toye looked at his paper. "No, I guess I'm wrong. Seems it happened Wednesday, but he only passed away Sunday morning."

Cazalet still sat staring at him—there was not room for two of them on their feet—but into his heavy stare there came a gleam of leaden wisdom. "This was Thursday morning," he said, "so I didn't dream of it when it happened, after all."

"You dreamed you saw him lying dead, and so he was," said Toye. "The funeral's been to-day. I don't know, but that seems to me just about the next nearest thing to seeing the crime perpetrated in a vision."

"Crime!" cried Cazalet. "What crime?"

"Murder, sir!" said Hilton Toye. "Wilful, brutal, bloody murder! Here's the paper; better read it for yourself. I'm glad he wasn't a friend of yours, or mine either, but it's a bad end even for your worst enemy."

The paper fluttered in Cazalet's clutch as it had done in Toye's; but that was as natural as his puzzled frown over the cryptic allusions of a journal that had dealt fully with the ascertainable facts in previous issues. Some few emerged between the lines. Henry Craven had received his fatal injuries on the Wednesday of the previous week. The thing had happened in his library, at or about half past seven in the evening; but how a crime, which was apparently a profound mystery, had been timed to within a minute of its commission did not appear among the latest particulars. No arrest had been made. No clue was mentioned, beyond the statement that the police were still searching for a definite instrument with which it was evidently assumed that the deed had been committed. There was in fact a close description of an unusual weapon, a special constable's very special truncheon. It had hung as a cherished trophy on the library wall, from which it was missing, while the very imprint of a silver shield, mounted on the thick end of the weapon, was stated to have been discovered on the scalp of the fractured skull. But that was a little bit of special reporting, typical of the enterprising sheet that Toye had procured. The inquest, merely opened on the Monday, had been adjourned to the day of issue.

"We must get hold of an evening paper," said Cazalet. "Fancy his own famous truncheon! He had it mounted and inscribed himself, so that it shouldn't be forgotten how he'd fought for law and order at Trafalgar Square! That was the man all over!"

His voice and manner achieved the excessive indifference which the English type holds due from itself after any excess of feeling. Toye also was himself again, his alert mind working keenly yet darkly in his acute eyes.

"I wonder if it was a murder?" he speculated. "I bet it wasn't a deliberate murder."

"What else could it have been?"

"Kind of manslaughter. Deliberate murderers don't trust to chance weapons hanging on their victims' walls."

"You forget," said Cazalet, "that he was robbed as well."

"Do they claim that?" said Hilton Toye. "I guess I skipped some. Where does it say anything about his being robbed?"

"Here!" Cazalet had scanned the paper eagerly; his finger drummed upon the place. "'The police,'" he read out, in some sort of triumph, "'have now been furnished with a full description of the missing watch and trinkets and the other articles believed to have been taken from the pockets of the deceased.' What's that but robbery?"

"You're dead right," said Toye. "I missed that somehow. Yet who in thunder tracks a man down to rob and murder him in his own home? But when you've brained a man, because you couldn't keep your hands off him, you might deliberately do all the rest to make it seem like the work of thieves."

Hilton Toye looked a judge of deliberation as he measured his irrefutable words. He looked something more. Cazalet could not tear his blue eyes from the penetrating pair that met them with a somber twinkle, an enlightened gusto, quite uncomfortably suggestive at such a moment.

"You aren't a detective, by any chance, are you?" cried Cazalet, with rather clumsy humor.

"No, sir! But I've often thought I wouldn't mind being one," said Toye, chuckling. "I rather figure I might do something at it. If things don't go my way in your old country, and they put up a big enough reward, why, here's a man I knew and a place I know, and I might have a mind to try my hand."

They went ashore together, and to the same hotel at Southampton for the night. Perhaps neither could have said from which side the initiative came; but midnight found the chance pair with their legs under the same heavy Victorian mahogany, devouring cold beef, ham and pickles as phlegmatically as commercial travelers who had never been off the island in their lives. Yet surely Cazalet was less depressed than he had been before landing; the old English ale in a pewter tankard even elicited a few of those anecdotes and piquant comparisons in which his conversation was at its best. It was at its worst on general questions, or on concrete topics not introduced by himself; and into this category, perhaps not unnaturally, fell such further particulars of the Thames Valley mystery as were to be found in an evening paper at the inn. They included a fragmentary report of the adjourned inquest, and the actual offer of such a reward, by the dead man's firm, for the apprehension of his murderer, as made Toye's eyes glisten in his sagacious head.

But Cazalet, though he had skimmed the many-headed column before sitting down to supper, flatly declined to discuss the tragedy his first night ashore.

------

# III
# IN THE TRAIN

Discussion was inevitable on the way up to town next morning.

The silly season was by no means over; a sensational inquest was worth every inch that it could fill in most of the morning papers; and the two strange friends, planted opposite each other in the first-class smoker, traveled inland simultaneously engrossed in a copious report of the previous day's proceedings at the coroner's court.

Of solid and significant fact, they learned comparatively little that they had been unable to gather or deduce the night before. There was the medical evidence, valuable only as tracing the fatal blow to some such weapon as the missing truncheon; there was the butler's evidence, finally timing the commission of the deed to within ten minutes; there was the head gardener's evidence, confirming and supplementing that of the butler; and there was the evidence of a footman who had answered the telephone an hour or two before the tragedy occurred.

The butler had explained that the dinner-hour was seven thirty; that, not five minutes before, he had seen his master come down-stairs and enter the library, where, at seven fifty-five, on going to ask if he had heard the gong, he had obtained no answer but found the door locked on the inside; that he had then hastened round by the garden, and in through the French window, to discover the deceased gentleman lying in his blood.

The head gardener, who lived in the lodge, had sworn to having seen a bareheaded man rush past his windows and out of the gates about the same hour, as he knew by the sounding of the gong up at the house; they often heard it at the lodge, in warm weather when the windows were open, and the gardener swore that he himself had heard it on this occasion.

The footman appeared to have been less positive as to the time of the telephone call, thought it was between four and five, but remembered the conversation very well. The gentleman had asked whether Mr. Craven was at home, had been told that he was out motoring, asked when he would be back, told he couldn't say, but before dinner some time, and what name should he give, whereupon the gentleman had rung off without answering. The footman thought he was a gentleman, from the way he spoke. But apparently the police had not yet succeeded in tracing the call.

"Is it a difficult thing to do?" asked Cazalet, touching on this last point early in the discussion, which even he showed no wish to avoid this morning. He had dropped his paper, to find that Toye had already dropped his, and was gazing at the flying English fields with thoughtful puckers about his somber eyes.

"If you ask me," he replied, "I should like to know what wasn't difficult connected with the telephone system in this country! Why, you don't have a system, and that's all there is to it. But it's not at that end they'll put the salt on their man."

"Which end will it be, then?"

"The river end. That hat, or cap. Do you see what the gardener says about the man who ran out bareheaded? That gardener deserves to be cashiered for not getting a move on him in time to catch that man, even if he did think he'd only been swiping flowers. But if he went and left his hat or his cap behind him, that should be good enough in the long run. It's the very worst thing you *can* leave. Ever hear of Franz Müller?"

Cazalet had not heard of that immortal notoriety, nor did his ignorance appear to trouble him at all, but it was becoming more and more clear that Hilton Toye took an almost unhealthy interest in the theory and practise of violent crime.

"Franz Müller," he continued, "left his hat behind him, only that and nothing more, but it brought him to the gallows even though he got over to the other side first. He made the mistake of taking a slow steamer, and that's just about the one mistake they never did make at Scotland Yard. Give them a nice, long, plain-sailing stern-chase and they get there by bedtime—wireless or no wireless!"

But Cazalet was in no mind to discuss other crimes, old or new; and he closed the digression by asserting somewhat roundly that neither hat nor cap had been left behind in the only case that interested him.

"Don't be too sure," said Toye. "Even Scotland Yard doesn't show all its hand at once, in the first inquiry that comes along. They don't give out any description of the man that ran away, but you bet it's being circulated around every police office in the United Kingdom."

Cazalet said they would give it out fast enough if they had it to give. By the way, he was surprised to see that the head gardener was the same who had been at Uplands in his father's time; he must be getting an old man, and no doubt shakier on points of detail than he would be likely to admit. Cazalet instanced the alleged hearing of the gong as in itself an unconvincing statement. It was well over a hundred yards from the gates to the house, and there were no windows to open in the hall where the gong would be rung.

He sighed heavily as in his turn he looked out at the luxuriant little paddocks and the old tiled homesteads after every two or three. But he was not thinking of the weather-board and corrugated iron strewn so sparsely over the yellow wilds that he had left behind him. The old English panorama flew by for granted, as he had taken it before ever he went out to Australia. It was as though he had never been out at all.

"I've dreamed of the old spot so often," he said at length. "I'm not thinking of the night before last—I meant in the bush—and now to think of a thing like this happening, there, in the old governor's den, of all places!"

"Seems like a kind of poetic justice," said Hilton Toye.

"It does. It is!" cried Cazalet, fetching moist yet fiery eyes in from the fields. "I said to you the other night that Henry Craven never was a white man, and I won't unsay it now. Nobody may ever know what he's done to bring this upon him. But those who really knew the man, and suffered for it, can guess the kind of thing!"

"Exactly," murmured Toye, as though he had just said as much himself. His dark eyes twinkled with deliberation and debate. "How long is it, by the way, that they gave that clerk and friend of yours?"

A keen look pressed the startling question; at least, it startled Cazalet.

"You mean Scruton? What on earth made you think of him?"

"Talking of those who suffered for being the dead man's friends, I guess," said Toye. "Was it fourteen years?"

"That was it."

"But I guess fourteen doesn't mean fourteen, ordinarily, if a prisoner behaves himself?"

"No, I believe not. In fact, it doesn't."

"Do you know how much it would mean?"

"A little more than ten."

"Then Scruton may be out now?"

"Just."

Toye nodded with detestable aplomb. "That gives you something to chew on," said he. "Of course, I don't say he's our man—"

"I should think you didn't!" cried Cazalet, white to the lips with sudden fury.

Toye looked disconcerted and distressed, but at the same time frankly puzzled. He apologized none the less readily, with almost ingenious courtesy and fulness, but he ended by explaining himself in a single sentence, and that told more than the rest of his straightforward eloquence put together.

"If a man had done you down like that, wouldn't you want to kill him the very moment you came out, Cazalet?"

The creature of impulse was off at a tangent. "I'd forgive him if he did it, too!" he exclaimed. "I'd move heaven and earth to save him, guilty or not guilty. Wouldn't you in my place?"

"I don't know," said Hilton Toye. "It depends on the place you're in, I guess!" And the keen dark eyes came drilling into Cazalet's skull like augers.

"I thought I told you?" he explained impatiently. "We were in the office together; he was good to me, winked at the business hours I was inclined to keep, let me down lighter in every way than I deserved. You may say it was part of his game. But I take people as I find them. And then, as I told you, Scruton was ten thousand times more sinned against than sinning."

"Are you sure? If you knew it at the time—"

"I didn't. I told you so the last night."

"Then it came to you in Australia?" said Toye, with a smile as whimsical as the suggestion.

"It did!" cried Cazalet unexpectedly. "In a letter," he added with hesitation.

"Well, I mustn't ask questions," said Hilton Toye, and began folding up his newspaper with even more than his usual deliberation.

"Oh, I'll tell you!" cried Cazalet ungraciously. "It's my own fault for telling you so much. It was in a letter from Scruton himself that I heard the whole thing. I'd written to him—toward the end—suggesting things. He managed to get an answer through that would never have passed the prison authorities. And—and that's why I came home just when I did," concluded Cazalet; "that's why I didn't wait till after shearing. He's been through about enough, and I've had more luck than I deserved. I meant to take him back with me, to keep the books on our station, if you want to know!" The brusk voice trembled.

Toye let his newspaper slide to the floor. "But that was fine!" he exclaimed simply. "That's as fine an action as I've heard of in a long time."

"If it comes off," said Cazalet in a gloomy voice.

"Don't you worry. It'll come off. Is he out yet, for sure? I mean, do you know

14

that he is?"

"Scruton? Yes—since you press it—he wrote to tell me that he was coming out even sooner than he expected."

"Then he can stop out for me," said Hilton Toye. "I guess I'm not running for that reward!"

———————

# IV
# DOWN THE RIVER

At Waterloo the two men parted, with a fair exchange of fitting speeches, none of which rang really false. And yet Cazalet found himself emphatically unable to make any plans at all for the next few days; also, he seemed in two minds now about a Jermyn Street hotel previously mentioned as his immediate destination; and his step was indubitably lighter as he went off first of all to the loop-line, to make sure of some train or other that he might have to take before the day was out.

In the event he did not take that train or any other; for the new miracle of the new traffic, the new smell of the horseless streets, and the newer joys of the newest of new taxicabs, all worked together and so swiftly upon Cazalet's organism that he had a little colloquy with his smart young driver instead of paying him in Jermyn Street. He nearly did pay him off, and with something more than his usual impetuosity, as either a liar or a fool with no sense of time or space.

"But that's as quick as the train, my good fellow!" blustered Cazalet.

"Quicker," said the smart young fellow without dipping his cigarette, "if you were going by the old Southwestern!"

The very man, and especially the manners that made or marred him, was entirely new to Cazalet as a product of the old country. But he had come from the bush, and he felt as though he might have been back there but for the smell of petrol and the cry of the motor-horn from end to end of those teeming gullies of bricks and mortar.

He had accompanied his baggage just as far as the bureau of the Jermyn Street hotel. Any room they liked, and he would be back some time before midnight; that was his card, they could enter his name for themselves. He departed, pipe in mouth, open knife in one hand, plug tobacco in the other; and remarks were passed in Jermyn Street as the taxi bounced out west in ballast.

But indeed it was too fine a morning to waste another minute indoors, even to change one's clothes, if Cazalet had possessed any better than the ones he wore and did not rather glory in his rude attire. He was not wearing leggings, and he did wear a collar, but he quite saw that even so he might have cut an ignominious figure on the flags of Kensington Gore; no, now it was the crowded High Street, and now it was humble Hammersmith. He had told his smart young man to be sure and go that way. He had been at St. Paul's school as a boy—with old Venus Potts—and he wanted to see as many landmarks as he could. This one towered and was gone as nearly in a flash as a great red mountain could. It seemed to Cazalet, but perhaps he expected it to seem, that the red was a little mellower, the ivy a good deal higher on the great warm walls. He noted the time by the ruthless old clock. It was after one already; he would miss his lunch. What did that matter?

Lunch?

Drunken men do not miss their meals, and Cazalet was simply and comfortably drunk with the delight of being back. He had never dreamed of its getting into his head like this; at the time he did not realize that it had. That was the beauty of his bout. He knew well enough what he was doing and seeing, but inwardly he was literally blind. Yesterday was left behind and forgotten like the Albert Memorial, and to-morrow was still as distant as the sea, if there were such things as to-morrow and the sea.

Meanwhile what vivid miles of dazzling life, what a subtle autumn flavor in the air; how cool in the shadows, how warm in the sun; what a sparkling old river it was, to be sure; and yet, if those weren't the first of the autumn tints on the trees in Castlenau.

There went a funeral, on its way to Mortlake! The taxi overhauled it at a callous speed. Cazalet just had time to tear off his great soft hat. It was actually the first funeral he had seen since his own father's; no wonder his radiance suffered a brief eclipse. But in another moment he was out on Barnes' Common. Then, in the Lower Richmond Road, the smart young man began to change speed and crawl, and at once there was something fresh to think about. The Venture and its team of grays, Oxford and London, was trying to pass a motor-bus just ahead, and a gray leader was behaving as though it also had just landed from the bush. Cazalet thought of a sailing-ship and a dreadnought, and the sailing-ship thrown up into the wind. Then he wondered how one of Cobb's bush coaches would have behaved, and thought it might have played the barge!

It had been the bicycle age when he went away; now it was the motor age, and the novelty and contrast were endless to a simple mind under the influence of forgotten yet increasingly familiar scenes. But nothing was lost on Cazalet that great morning; even a milk-float entranced him, itself enchanted, with its tall can turned to gold and silver in the sun. But now he was on all but holy ground. It was not so holy with these infernal electric trams; still he knew every inch of it; and now, thank goodness, he was off the lines at last.

"Slower!" he shouted to his smart young man. He could not say that no notice was taken of the command. But a wrought-iron gate on the left, with a covered way leading up to the house, and the garden (that he could not see) leading down to the river, and the stables (that he could) across the road—all that was past and gone in a veritable twinkling. And though he turned round and looked back, it was only to get a sightless stare from sightless windows, to catch on a board "*This Delightful Freehold Residence with Grounds and Stabling*," and to echo the epithet with an appreciative grunt.

Five or six minutes later the smart young man was driving really slowly along a narrow road between patent wealth and blatant semi-gentility; on the left good grounds, shaded by cedar and chestnut, and on the right a row of hideous little houses, as pretentious as any that ever let for forty pounds within forty minutes of Waterloo.

"This can't be it!" shouted Cazalet. "It can't be here—stop! *Stop!* I tell you!"

A young woman had appeared in one of the overpowering wooden porticoes; two or three swinging strides were bringing her down the silly little path to the wicket-gate with the idiotic name; there was no time to open it before Cazalet blundered up, and shot his hand across to get a grasp as firm and friendly as he gave.

"Blanchie!"

"Sweep!"

They were their two nursery names, hers no improvement on the proper monosyllable, and his a rather dubious token of pristine proclivities. But out both came as if they were children still, and children who had been just long enough apart to start with a good honest mutual stare.

"You aren't a bit altered," declared the man of thirty-three, with a note not entirely tactful in his admiring voice. But his old chum only laughed.

"Fiddle!" she cried. "But you're not altered enough. Sweep, I'm disappointed in you. Where's your beard?"

"I had it off the other day. I always meant to," he explained, "before the end of the voyage. I wasn't going to land like a wild man of the woods, you know!"

"Weren't you! I call it mean."

Her scrutiny became severe, but softened again at the sight of his clutched wide-awake and curiously characterless, shapeless suit.

"You may well look!" he cried, delighted that she should. "They're awful old duds, I know, but you would think them a wonder if you saw where they came

18

from: a regular roadside shanty in a forsaken township at the back of beyond. Extraordinary cove, the chap who made them; puts in every stitch himself, learns Shakespeare while he's at it, knew Lindsay Gordon and Marcus Clarke —"

"I'm sorry to interrupt," said Blanche, laughing, "but there's your taxi ticking up twopence every quarter of an hour, and I can't let it go on without warning you. Where have you come from?"

He told her with a grin, was roundly reprimanded for his extravagance, but brazened it out by giving the smart young man a sovereign before her eyes. After that, she said he had better come in before the neighbors came out and mobbed him for a millionaire. And he followed her indoors and up-stairs, into a little new den crowded with some of the big old things he could remember in a very different setting. But if the room was small it had a balcony that was hardly any smaller, on top of that unduly imposing porch; and out there, overlooking the fine grounds opposite, were basket chairs and a table, hot with the Indian summer sun.

"I hope you are not shocked at my abode," said Blanche. "I'm afraid I can't help it if you are. It's just big enough for Martha and me; you remember old Martha, don't you? You'll have to come and see her, but she'll be horribly disappointed about your beard!"

Coming through the room, stopping to greet a picture and a bookcase (filling a wall each) as old friends, Cazalet had descried a photograph of himself with that appendage. He had threatened to take the beastly thing away, and Blanche had told him he had better not. But it did not occur to Cazalet that it was the photograph to which Hilton Toye had referred, or that Toye must have been in this very room to see it. In these few hours he had forgotten the man's existence, at least in so far as it associated itself with Blanche Macnair.

"The others all wanted me to live near them," she continued, "but as no two of them are in the same county it would have meant a caravan. Besides, I wasn't going to be transplanted at my age. Here one has everybody one ever knew, except those who escape by emigrating, simply at one's mercy on a bicycle. There's more golf and tennis than I can find time to play; and I still keep the old boat in the old boat-house at Littleford, because it hasn't let or sold yet, I'm sorry to say."

"So I saw as I passed," said Cazalet. "That board hit me hard!"

"The place being empty hits me harder," rejoined the last of the Macnairs. "It's going down in value every day like all the other property about here, except this sort. Mind where you throw that match, Sweep! I don't want you to set fire to my pampas-grass; it's the only tree I've got!"

Cazalet laughed; she was making him laugh quite often. But the pampas-grass, like the rest of the ridiculous little garden in front, was obscured if not overhung by the balcony on which they sat. And the subject seemed one to change.

"It was simply glorious coming down," he said. "I wouldn't swap that three-quarters of an hour for a bale of wool; but, I say, there are some changes! The whole show in the streets is different. I could have spotted it with my eyes and ears shut. They used to smell like a stable, and now they smell like a lamp. And I used to think the old cabbies could drive, but their job was child's play to the taximan's! We were at Hammersmith before I could light my pipe, and almost down here before it went out! But you can't think how every mortal thing on the way appealed to me. The only blot was a funeral at Barnes; it seemed such a sin to be buried on a day like this, and a fellow like me just coming home to enjoy himself!"

He had turned grave, but not graver than at the actual moment coming down. Indeed, he was simply coming down again, for her benefit and his own, without an ulterior trouble until Blanche took him up with a long face of her own.

"We've had a funeral here. I suppose you know?"

"Yes. I know."

Her chair creaked as she leaned forward with an enthusiastic solemnity that would have made her shriek if she had seen herself; but it had no such effect on Cazalet.

"I wonder who can have done it!"

"So do the police, and they don't look much like finding out!"

"It must have been for his watch and money, don't you think? And yet they say he had so many enemies!" Cazalet kept silence; but she thought he winced. "Of course it must have been the man who ran out of the drive," she concluded hastily. "Where were you when it happened, Sweep?"

Somewhat hoarsely he was recalling the Mediterranean movements of the *Kaiser Fritz*, when at the first mention of the vessel's name he was firmly heckled.

"Sweep, you *don't* mean to say you came by a German steamer?"

"I do. It was the first going, and why should I waste a week? Besides, you can generally get a cabin to yourself on the German line."

"So that's why you're here before the end of the month," said Blanche. "Well, I call it most unpatriotic; but the cabin to yourself was certainly some excuse."

"That reminds me!" he exclaimed. "I hadn't it to myself all the way; there was another fellow in with me from Genoa; and the last night on board it came out that he knew you!"

"*Who* can it have been?"

"Toye, his name was. Hilton Toye."

"An American man! Oh, but I know him very well," said Blanche in a tone both strained and cordial. "He's great fun, Mr. Toye, with his delightful Americanisms, and the perfectly delightful way he says them!"

Cazalet puckered like the primitive man he was, when taken at all by surprise; and that anybody, much less Blanche, should think Toye, of all people, either "delightful" or "great fun" was certainly a surprise to him, if it was nothing else. Of course it was nothing else, to his immediate knowledge; still, he was rather ready to think that Blanche was blushing, but forgot, if indeed he had been in a fit state to see it at the time, that she had paid himself the same high compliment across the gate. On the whole, it may be said that Cazalet was ruffled without feeling seriously disturbed as to the essential issue which alone leaped to his mind.

"Where did you meet the fellow?" he inquired, with the suitable admixture of confidence and amusement.

"In the first instance, at Engelberg."

"Engelberg! Where's that?"

"Only one of those places in Switzerland where everybody goes nowadays for what they call winter sports."

She was not even smiling at his arrogant ignorance; she was merely explaining one geographical point and another of general information. A close observer might have thought her almost anxious not to identify herself too closely with a popular craze.

"I dare say you mentioned it," said Cazalet, but rather as though he was wondering why she had not.

"I dare say I didn't! Everything won't go into an annual letter. It was the winter before last—I went out with Betty and her husband."

"And after that he took a place down here?"

"Yes. Then I met him on the river the following summer, and found he'd got rooms in one of the Nell Gwynne Cottages, if you call that a place."

"I see."

But there was no more to see; there never had been much, but now Blanche was standing up and gazing out of the balcony into the belt of singing sunshine between the opposite side of the road and the invisible river acres away.

"Why shouldn't we go down to Littleford and get out the boat if you're really going to make an afternoon of it?" she said. "But you simply must see Martha first; and while she's making herself fit to be seen, you must take something for the good of the house. I'll bring it to you on a lordly tray."

She brought him siphon, stoppered bottle, a silver biscuit-box of ancient memories, and left him alone with them some little time; for the young mistress, like her old retainer in another minute, was simply dying to make herself more presentable. Yet when she had done so, and came back like snow, in a shirt and skirt just home from the laundry, she saw that he did not see the difference. His devouring eyes shone neither more nor less; but he had also devoured every biscuit in the box, though he had begun by vowing that he had lunched in town, and stuck to the fable still.

Old Martha had known him all his life, but best at the period when he used to come to nursery tea at Littleford. She declared she would have known him anywhere as he was, but she simply hadn't recognized him in that photograph with his beard.

"I can see where it's been," said Martha, looking him in the lower temperate zone. "But I'm so glad you've had it off, Mr. Cazalet."

"There you are, Blanchie!" crowed Cazalet. "You said she'd be disappointed, but Martha's got better taste."

"It isn't that, sir," said Martha earnestly. "It's because the dreadful man who was seen running out of the drive, at your old home, *he* had a beard! It's in all the notices about him, and that's what's put me against them, and makes me glad you've had yours off."

Blanche turned to him with too ready a smile; but then she was really not such a great age as she pretended, and she had never been in better spirits in her life.

"You hear, Sweep! I call it rather lucky for you that you were—"

But just then she saw his face, and remembered the things that had been said about Henry Craven by the Cazalets' friends, even ten years ago, when she really had been a girl.

# V
# AN UNTIMELY VISITOR

She really was one still, for in these days it is an elastic term, and in Blanche's case there was no apparent reason why it should ever cease to apply, or to be applied by every decent tongue except her own. If, however, it be conceded that she herself had reached the purely mental stage of some self-consciousness on the point of girlhood, it can not be too clearly stated that it was the only point in which Blanche Macnair had ever been self-conscious in her life.

Much the best tennis-player among the ladies of the neighborhood, she drove an almost unbecomingly long ball at golf, and never looked better than when paddling her old canoe, or punting in the old punt. And yet, this wonderful September afternoon, she did somehow look even better than at either or any of those congenial pursuits, and that long before they reached the river; in the empty house, which had known her as baby, child and grown-up girl, to the companion of some part of all three stages, she looked a more lustrous and a lovelier Blanche than he remembered even of old.

But she was not really lovely in the least; that also must be put beyond the pale of misconception. Her hair was beautiful, and perhaps her skin, and, in some lights, her eyes; the rest was not. It was yellow hair, not golden, and Cazalet would have given all he had about him to see it down again as in the oldest of old days; but there was more gold in her skin, for so the sun had treated it; and there was even hint or glint (in certain lights, be it repeated) of gold mingling with the pure hazel of her eyes. But in the dusty shadows of the empty house, moving like a sunbeam across its bare boards, standing out against the discolored walls in the place of remembered pictures not to be compared with her, it was there that she was all golden and still a girl.

They poked their noses into the old bogy-hole under the nursery stairs; they swung the gate at the head of the next flight; they swore to finger-marks on the panels that were all the walls of the top story, and they had a laugh in every corner, childish crimes to reconstruct, quite bitter battles to fight over again, but never a lump in either throat that the other could have guessed was there. And so out upon the leafy lawn, shelving abruptly to the river; round first, however, to the drying-green where the caretakers' garments were indeed drying unashamed; but they knew each other well enough to laugh aloud, had picked each other up much farther back than the point of parting ten years ago, almost as far as the days of mixed cricket with a toy set, on that very green.

Then there was the poor old greenhouse, sagging in every slender timber, broken as to every other cobwebbed pane, empty and debased within; they could not bring themselves to enter here.

Last of all there was the summer schoolroom over the boat-house, quite apart from the house itself; scene of such safe yet reckless revels; in its very aura late Victorian!

It lay hidden in ivy at the end of a now neglected path; the bow-windows overlooking the river were framed in ivy, like three matted, whiskered, dirty, happy faces; one, with its lower sash propped open by a broken plant-pot, might have been grinning a toothless welcome to two once leading spirits of the place.

Cazalet whittled a twig and wedged that sash up altogether; then he sat himself on the sill, his long legs inside. But his knife had reminded him of his plug tobacco. And his plug tobacco took him as straight back to the bush as though the unsound floor had changed under their feet into a magic carpet.

"You simply have it put down to the man's account in the station books. Nobody keeps ready money up at the bush, not even the price of a plug like this; but the chap I'm telling you about (I can see him now, with his great red beard and freckled fists) he swore I was charging him for half a pound more than he'd ever had. I was station storekeeper, you see; it was quite the beginning of things, and I'd have had to pay the few bob myself, and be made to look so small that I shouldn't have had a soul to call my own on the run. So I fought him for the difference; we fought for twenty minutes behind the wood-heap; then he gave me best, but I had to turn in till I could see again."

"You don't mean that he——"

Blanche had looked rather disgusted the moment before; now she was all truculent suspense and indignation.

"Beat me?" he cried. "Good Lord, no; but there was none too much in it."

Fires died down in her hazel eyes, lay lambent as soft moonlight, flickered into laughter before he had seen the fire.

"I'm afraid you're a very dangerous person," said Blanche.

"You've got to be," he assured her; "it's the only way. Don't take a word from anybody, unless you mean him to wipe his boots on you. I soon found that out. I'd have given something to have learned the noble art before I went out. Did I ever tell you how it was I first came across old Venus Potts?"

He had told her at great length, to the exclusion of about every other topic, in the second of the annual letters; and throughout the series the inevitable name of Venus Potts had seldom cropped up without some allusion to that Homeric encounter. But it was well worth while having it all over again with the intricate and picaresque embroidery of a tongue far mightier than the pen hitherto employed upon the incident. Poor Blanche had almost to hold her nose over the primary cause of battle; but the dialogue was delightful, and Cazalet himself made a most gallant and engaging figure as he sat on the sill and reeled it out. He had always been a fluent teller of any happening, and Blanche a ready commentator, capable of raising the general level of the entertainment at any moment. But after all these centuries it was fun enough to listen as long as he liked to go on; and perhaps she saw that he had more scope where they were than he could have had in the boat, or it may have been an unrealized spell that bound them both to their bare old haunt; but there they were a good twenty minutes later, and old Venus Potts was still on the magic *tapis*, though Cazalet had dropped his boasting for a curiously humble, eager and yet ineffectual vein.

"Old Venus Potts!" he kept ejaculating. "You couldn't help liking him. And he'd like you, my word!"

"Is his wife nice?" Blanche wanted to know; but she was looking so intently out her window, at the opposite end of the bow to Cazalet's, that a man of the wider world might have thought of something else to talk about.

Out her window she looked past a willow that had been part of the old life, in the direction of an equally typical silhouette of patient anglers anchored in a punt; they had not raised a rod between them during all this time that Blanche had been out in Australia; but as a matter of fact she never saw them, since, vastly to the credit of Cazalet's descriptive powers, she was out in Australia still.

"Nelly Potts?" he said. "Oh, a jolly good sort; you'd be awful pals."

"Should we?" said Blanche, just smiling at her invisible anglers.

"I know you would," he assured her with immense conviction. "Of course she can't do the things you do; but she can ride, my word! So she ought to, when she's lived there all her life. The rooms aren't much, but the verandas are what count most; they're better than any rooms. There are two distinct ends to the station—it's like two houses; but of course the barracks were good enough just for me."

She knew about the bachelors' barracks; the annual letter had been really very full; and then she was still out there, cultivating Nelly Potts on a very deep veranda, though her straw hat and straw hair remained in contradictory evidence against a very dirty window on the Middlesex bank of the Thames.

It was a shame of the September sun to show the dirt as it was doing; not only was there a great steady pool of sunlight on the unspeakable floor, but a doddering reflection from the river on the disreputable ceiling. Cazalet looked rather desperately from one to the other, and both the calm pool and the rough were broken by shadows, one more impressionistic than the other, of a straw hat over a stack of straw hair, that had not gone out to Australia—yet.

And of course just then a step sounded outside somewhere on some gravel. Confound those caretakers! What were *they* doing, prowling about?

"I say, Blanchie!" he blurted out. "I do believe you'd like it out there, a sportswoman like you! I believe you'd take to it like a duck to water."

He had floundered to his feet as well. He was standing over her, feeling his way like a great fatuous coward, so some might have thought. But it really looked as though Blanche was not attending to what he did say; yet neither was she watching her little anglers stamped in jet upon a silvery stream, nor even seeing any more of Nelly Potts in the Australian veranda. She had come home from Australia, and come in from the river, and she was watching the open door at the other end of the old schoolroom, listening to those confounded steps coming nearer and nearer—and Cazalet was gazing at her as though he really had said something that deserved an answer.

"Why, Miss Blanche!" cried a voice. "And your old lady-in-waiting figured I should find you flown!"

Hilton Toye was already a landsman and a Londoner from top to toe. He was perfectly dressed—for Bond Street—and his native simplicity of bearing and address placed him as surely and firmly in the present picture. He did not look the least bit out of it. But Cazalet did, in an instant; his old bush clothes changed at once into a merely shabby suit of despicable cut; the romance dropped out of them and their wearer, as he stood like a trussed turkey-cock, and watched a bunch of hothouse flowers presented to the lady with a little gem of a natural, courteous, and yet characteristically racy speech.

To the lady, mark you; for she was one, on the spot; and Cazalet was a man again, and making a mighty effort to behave himself because the hour of boy and girl was over.

"Mr. Cazalet," said Toye, "I guess you want to know what in thunder I'm doing on your tracks so soon. It's hog-luck, sir, because I wanted to see you quite a lot, but I never thought I'd strike you right here. Did you hear the news?"

"No! What?"

There was no need to inquire as to the class of news; the immediate past had come back with Toye into Cazalet's life; and even in Blanche's presence, even in her schoolroom, the old days had flown into their proper place and size in the perspective.

"They've made an arrest," said Toye; and Cazalet nodded as though he had quite expected it, which set Blanche off trying to remember something he had said at the other house; but she had not succeeded when she noticed the curious pallor of his chin and forehead.

"Scruton?" he just asked.

"Yes, sir! This morning," said Hilton Toye.

"You don't mean *the* poor man?" cried Blanche, looking from one to the other.

"Yes, he does," said Cazalet gloomily. He stared out at the river, seeing nothing in his turn, though one of the anglers was actually busy with his reel.

"But I thought Mr. Scruton was still—" Blanche remembered him, remembered dancing with him; she did not like to say, "in prison."

"He came out the other day," sighed Cazalet. "But how like the police all over! Give a dog a bad name, and trust them to hunt it down and shoot it at sight!"

"I judge it's not so bad as all that in this country," said Hilton Toye. "That's more like the police theory about Scruton, I guess, bar drawing the bead."

"When did you hear of it?" said Cazalet.

"It was on the tape at the Savoy when I got there. So I made an inquiry, and I figured to look in at the Kingston Court on my way to call upon Miss Blanche. You see, I was kind of interested in all you'd told me about the case."

"Well?"

"Well, that was my end of the situation. As luck and management would have it between them, I was in time to hear your man—"

"Not my man, please! You thought of him yourself," said Cazalet sharply.

"Well, anyway, I was in time to hear the proceedings opened against him. They were all over in about a minute. He was remanded till next week."

"How did he look?" and, "Had he a beard?" demanded Cazalet and Blanche simultaneously.

"He looked like a sick man," said Toye, with something more than his usual deliberation in answering or asking questions. "Yes, Miss Blanche, he had a beard worthy of a free citizen."

"They let them grow one, if they like, before they come out," said Cazalet, with the nod of knowledge.

"Then I guess he was a wise man not to take it off," rejoined Hilton Toye. "That would only prejudice his case, if it's going to be one of identity, with that head gardener playing lead in the witness-stand."

"Old Savage!" snorted Cazalet. "Why, he was a dotard in our time; they couldn't hang a dog on his evidence!"

"Still," said Blanche, "I'd rather have it than circumstantial evidence, wouldn't you, Mr. Toye?"

"No, Miss Blanche, I would not," replied Toye, with unhesitating candor. "The worst evidence in the world, in my opinion, and I've given the matter some thought, is the evidence of identity." He turned to Cazalet, who had betrayed a quickened interest in his views. "Shall I tell you why? Think how often you're not so sure if you have seen a man before or if you never have! You kind of shrink from nodding, or else you nod wrong; if you didn't ever have that feeling, then you're not like any other man I know."

"I have!" cried Cazalet. "I've had it all my life, even in the wilds; but I never thought of it before."

"Think of it now," said Toye, "and you'll see there may be flaws in the best evidence of identity that money can buy. But circumstantial evidence can't lie, Miss Blanche, if you get enough of it. If the links fit in, to prove that a certain person was in a certain place at a certain time, I guess that's worth all the oaths of all the eye-witnesses that ever saw daylight!"

Cazalet laughed harshly, as for no apparent reason he led the way into the garden. "Mr. Toye's made a study of these things," he fired over his shoulder. "He should have been a Sherlock Holmes, and rather wishes he was one!"

"Give me time," said Toye, laughing. "I may come along that way yet."

Cazalet faced him in a frame of tangled greenery. "You told me you wouldn't!"

"I did, sir, but that was before they put salt on this poor old crook. If you're right, and he's not the man, shouldn't you say that rather altered the situation?"

# VI
# VOLUNTARY SERVICE

"And why do you think he can't have done it?"

Cazalet had trundled the old canoe over the rollers, and Blanche was hardly paddling in the glassy strip alongside the weir. Big drops clustered on her idle blades, and made tiny circles as they met themselves in the shining mirror. But below the lock there had been something to do, and Blanche had done it deftly and silently, with almost equal capacity and grace. It had given her a charming flush and sparkle; and, what with the sun's bare hand on her yellow hair, she now looked even bonnier than indoors, yet not quite, quite such a girl. But then every bit of the boy had gone out of Cazalet. So that hour stolen from the past was up forever.

"Why do the police think the other thing?" he retorted. "What have they got to go on? That's what I want to know. I agree with Toye in one thing." Blanche looked up quickly. "I wouldn't trust old Savage an inch. I've been thinking about him and his precious evidence. Do you realize that it's quite dark now soon after seven? It was pretty thick saying his man was bareheaded, with neither hat nor cap left behind to prove it! Yet now it seems he's put a beard to him, and next we shall have the color of his eyes!"

Blanche laughed at his vigor of phrase; this was more like the old, hot-tempered, sometimes rather overbearing Sweep. Something had made him jump to the conclusion that Scruton could not possibly have killed Mr. Craven, whatever else he might have done in days gone by. So it simply *was* impossible, and anybody who took the other side, or had a word to say for the police, as a force not unknown to look before it leaped, would have to reckon henceforth with Sweep Cazalet.

Mr. Toye already had reckoned with him, in a little debate begun outside the old summer schoolroom at Littleford, and adjourned rather than finished at the iron gate into the road. In her heart of hearts Blanche could not say that Cazalet had the best of the argument, except, indeed, in the matter of heated emphasis and scornful asseveration. It was difficult, however, to know what line he really took; for while he scouted the very notion of uncorroborated identification by old Savage, he discredited with equal warmth all Toye's contentions on behalf of circumstantial evidence. Toye had advanced a general principle with calm ability, but Cazalet could not be shifted from the particular position he was so eager to defend, and would only enter into abstract questions to beg them out of hand.

Blanche rather thought that neither quite understood what the other meant; but she could not blink the fact that the old friend had neither the dialectical mind nor the unfailing courtesy of the new. That being so, with her perception she might have changed the subject; but she could see that Cazalet was thinking of nothing else; and no wonder, since they were approaching the scene of the tragedy and his own old home, with each long dip of her paddle.

It had been his own wish to start upstream; but she could see the wistful pain in his eyes as they fell once more upon the red turrets and the smooth green lawn of Uplands; and she neither spoke nor looked at him again until he spoke to her.

"I see they've got the blinds down still," he said detachedly. "What's happened to Mrs. Craven?"

"I hear she went into a nursing home before the funeral."

"Then there's nobody there?"

"It doesn't look as if there was, does it?" said poor Blanche.

"I expect we should find Savage somewhere. Would you very much mind, Blanche? I should rather like—if it was just setting foot—with you—"

But even that effective final pronoun failed to bring any buoyancy back into his voice; for it was not in the least effective as he said it, and he no longer looked her in the face. But this all seemed natural to Blanche, in the manifold and overlapping circumstances of the case. She made for the inlet at the upper end of the lawn. And her prompt unquestioning acquiescence shamed Cazalet into further and franker explanation, before he could let her land to please him.

"You don't know how I feel this!" he exclaimed quite miserably. "I mean about poor old Scruton; he's gone through so much as it is, whatever he may have done to deserve it long ago. And he wasn't the only one, or the worst; some day I'll tell you how I know, but you may take it from me that's so. The real villain's gone to his account. I won't pretend I'm sorry for him. *De mortuis* doesn't apply if you've got to invent the *bonum*! But Scruton—after ten years—only think of it! Is it conceivable that he should go and do a thing like this the very moment he gets out? I ask you, is it even conceivable?"

He asked her with something of the ferocity with which he had turned on Toye for suggesting that the police might have something up their sleeves, and be given a chance. But Blanche understood him. And now she showed herself golden to the core, almost as an earnest of her fitness for the fires before her.

"Poor fellow," she cried, "he has a friend in you, at any rate! And I'll help you to help him, if there's any way I can?"

He clutched her hand, but only as he might have clutched a man's.

"You can't do anything; but I won't forget that," he almost choked. "I meant to stand by him in a very different way. He'd been down to the depths, and I'd come up a bit; then he was good to me as a lad, and it was my father's partner who was the ruin of him. I seemed to owe him something, and now—now I'll stand by him whatever happens and—whatever *has* happened!"

Then they landed in the old, old inlet. Cazalet knew every knot in the post to which he tied Blanche's canoe.

It was a very different place, this Uplands, from poor old Littleford on the lower reach. The grounds were five or six acres instead of about one, and a house in quite another class stood farther back from the river and very much farther from the road.

The inlet began the western boundary, which continued past the boat-house in the shape of a high hedge, a herbaceous border (not what it had been in the old days), and a gravel path. This path was screened from the lawn by a bank of rhododendrons, as of course were the back yard and kitchen premises, past which it led into the front garden, eventually debouching into the drive. It was the path along which Cazalet led the way this afternoon, and Blanche at his heels was so struck by something that she could not help telling him he knew his way very well.

"Every inch of it!" he said bitterly. "But so I ought, if anybody does."

"But these rhododendrons weren't here in your time. They're the one improvement. Don't you remember how the path ran round to the other end of the yard? This gate into it wasn't made."

"No more it was," said Cazalet, as they came up to the new gate on the right. It was open, and looking through they could see where the old gateway had been bricked. The rhododendrons topped the yard wall at that point, masking it from the lawn, and making on the whole an improvement of which anybody but a former son of the house might have taken more account.

He said he could see no other change. He pretended to recognize the very blinds that were down and flapping in the kitchen windows facing west. But for the fact that these windows were wide open, the whole place seemed as deserted as Littleford; but just past the windows, and flush with them, was the tradesmen's door, and the two trespassers were barely abreast of it when this door opened and disgorged a man.

The man was at first sight a most incongruous figure for the back premises of any house, especially in the country. He was tall, rather stout, very powerfully built and rather handsome in his way; his top-hat shone like his patent-leather boots, and his gray cutaway suit hung well in front and was duly creased as to the trousers; yet not for one moment was this personage in the picture, in the sense in which Hilton Toye had stepped into the Littleford picture.

"May I ask what you're doing here?" he demanded bluntly of the male intruder.

"No harm, I hope," replied Cazalet, smiling, much to his companion's relief. She had done him an injustice, however, in dreading an explosion when they were both obviously in the wrong, and she greatly admired the tone he took so readily. "I know we've no business here whatever; but it happens to be my old home, and I only landed from Australia last night. I'm on the river for the first time, and simply had to have a look round."

The other big man had looked far from propitiated by the earlier of these remarks, but the closing sentences had worked a change.

"Are you young Mr. Cazalet?" he cried.

"I am, or rather I was," laughed Cazalet, still on his mettle.

"You've read all about the case then, I don't mind betting!" exclaimed the other with a jerk of his topper toward the house behind him.

"I've read all I found in the papers last night and this morning, and such arrears as I've been able to lay my hands on," said Cazalet. "But, as I tell you, my ship only got in from Australia last night, and I came round all the way in her. There was nothing in the English papers when we touched at Genoa."

"I see, I see." The man was still looking him up and down. "Well, Mr. Cazalet, my name's Drinkwater, and I'm from Scotland Yard. I happen to be in charge of the case."

"I guessed as much," said Cazalet, and this surprised Blanche more than anything else from him. Yet nothing about him was any longer like the Sweep of other days, or of any previous part of that very afternoon. And this was also easy to understand on reflection; for if he meant to stand by the hapless Scruton, guilty or not guilty, he could not perhaps begin better than by getting on good terms with the police. But his ready tact, and in that case cunning, were certainly a revelation to one who had known him marvelously as boy and youth.

"I mustn't ask questions," he continued, "but I see you're still searching for things, Mr. Drinkwater."

"Still minding our own job," said Mr. Drinkwater genially. They had sauntered on with him to the corner of the house, and seen a bowler hat bobbing in the shrubbery down the drive. Cazalet laughed like a man.

"Well, I needn't tell you I know every inch of the old place," he said; "that is, barring alterations," as Blanche caught his eye. "But I expect this search is harrowed, rather?"

"Rather," said Mr. Drinkwater, standing still in the drive. He had also taken out a presentation gold half-hunter, suitably inscribed in memory of one of his more bloodless victories. But Cazalet could always be obtuse, and now he refused to look an inch lower than the detective-inspector's bright brown eyes.

"There's just one place that's occurred to me, Mr. Drinkwater, that perhaps may not have occurred to you."

"Where's that, Mr. Cazalet?"

"In the room where—the room itself."

Mr. Drinkwater's long stare ended in an indulgent smile. "You can show me if you like," said he indifferently. "But I suppose you know we've got the man?"

---

34

# VII
# AFTER MICHELANGELO

"I was thinking of his cap," said Cazalet, but only as they returned to the tradesmen's door, and just as Blanche put in her word, "What about me?"

Mr. Drinkwater eyed the trim white figure standing in the sun. "The more the merrier!" his grim humor had it. "I dare say you'll be able to teach us a thing or two as well, miss."

She could not help nudging Cazalet in recognition of this shaft. But Cazalet did not look round; he had now set foot in his old home.

It was all strangely still and inactive, as though domestic animation had been suspended indefinitely. Yet the open kitchen door revealed a female form in mufti; a sullen face looked out of the pantry as they passed; and through the old green door (only now it was a red one) they found another bowler hat bent over a pink paper at the foot of the stairs. There was a glitter of eyes under the bowler's brim as Mr. Drinkwater conducted his friends into the library.

The library was a square room of respectable size, but very close and dim with the one French window closed and curtained. But Mr. Drinkwater shut the door as well, and added indescribably to the lighting and atmospheric effects by switching on all the electric lamps; they burned sullenly in the partial daylight, exposed as thin angry bunches of red-hot wire in dusty bulbs.

The electric light had been put in by the Cravens; all the other fixtures in the room were as Cazalet remembered them. The bookshelves contained different books, and now there were no busts on top. Certain cupboards, grained and varnished in Victorian days, were undeniably improved by being enameled white.

But the former son of the house gave himself no time to waste in sentimental comparisons. He tapped a pair of mahogany doors, like those of a wardrobe let into the wall.

"Have you looked in here?" demanded Cazalet in yet another key. His air was almost authoritative now. Blanche could not understand it, but the experienced Mr. Drinkwater smiled his allowances for a young fellow on his native heath, after more years in the wilderness than were good for young fellows.

"What's the use of looking in a cigar cupboard?" that dangerous man of the world made mild inquiry.

"Cigar cupboard!" echoed Cazalet in disgust. "Did he really only use it for his cigars?"

"A cigar cupboard," repeated Drinkwater, "and locked up at the time it happened. What was it, if I may ask, in Mr. Cazalet's time?"

"I remember!" came suddenly from Blanche; but Cazalet only said, "Oh, well, if you know it was locked there's an end of it."

Drinkwater went to the door and summoned his subordinate. "Just fetch that chap from the pantry, Tom," said he; but the sullen sufferer from police rule took his time, in spite of them, and was sharply rated when he appeared.

"I thought you told me this was a cigar cupboard?" continued Drinkwater, in the browbeating tone of his first words to Cazalet outside.

"So it is," said the man.

"Then where's the key?"

"How should I know? *I* never kept it!" cried the butler, crowing over his oppressor for a change. "He would keep it on his own bunch; find his watch, and all the other things that were missing from his pockets when your men went through 'em, and you may find his keys, too!"

Drinkwater gave his man a double signal; the door slammed on a petty triumph for the servants' hall; but now both invaders remained within.

"Try your hand on it, Tom," said the superior officer. "I'm a free-lance here," he explained somewhat superfluously to the others, as Tom applied himself to the lock in one mahogany door. "Man's been drinking, I should say. He'd better be careful, because I don't take to him, drunk or sober. I'm not surprised at his master not trusting him. It's just possible that the place *was* open—he might have been getting out his cigars before dinner—but I can't say I think there's much in it, Mr. Cazalet."

It was open again—broken open—before many minutes; and certainly there was not much in it, to be seen, except cigars. Boxes of these were stacked on what might have been meant for a shallow desk (the whole place was shallow as the wardrobe that the doors suggested, but lighted high up at one end by a little barred window of its own) and according to Cazalet a desk it had really been. His poor father ought never to have been a business man; he ought to have been a poet. Cazalet said this now as simply as he had said it to Hilton Toye on board the *Kaiser Fritz*. Only he went rather farther for the benefit of the gentlemen from Scotland Yard, who took not the faintest interest in the late Mr. Cazalet, beyond poking their noses into his diminutive sanctum and duly turning them up at what they saw.

"He used to complain that he was never left in peace on Saturdays and Sundays, which of course were his only quiet times for writing," said the son, elaborating his tale with filial piety. "So once when I'd been trying to die of scarlet fever, and my mother brought me back from Hastings after she'd had me there some time, the old governor told us he'd got a place where he could disappear from the district at a moment's notice and yet be back in another moment if we rang the gong. I fancy he'd got to tell her where it was, pretty quick; but I only found out for myself by accident. Years afterward, he told me he'd got the idea from Jean Ingelow's place in Italy somewhere."

"It's in Florence," said Blanche, laughing. "I've been there and seen it, and it's the exact same thing. But you mean Michelangelo, Sweep!"

"Oh, do I?" he said serenely. "Well, I shall never forget how I found out its existence."

"No more shall I. You told me all about it at the time, as a terrific secret, and I may tell you that I've kept it from that day to this!"

"You would," he said simply. "But think of having the nerve to pull up the governor's floor! It only shows what a boy will do. I wonder if the hole's there still!"

Now all the time the planetary detective had been watching his satellite engaged in an attempt to render the damage done to the mahogany doors a little less conspicuous. Neither appeared to be taking any further interest in the cigar cupboard, or paying the slightest attention to Cazalet's reminiscences. But Mr. Drinkwater happened to have heard every word, and in the last sentence there was one that caused him to prick up his expert ears instinctively.

"What's that about a hole?" said he, turning round.

"I was reminding Miss Macnair how the place first came to be——"

"Yes, yes. But what about some hole in the floor?"

"I made one myself with one of those knives that contain all sorts of things, including a saw. It was one Saturday afternoon in the summer holidays. I came in here from the garden as my father went out by that door into the hall, leaving one of these mahogany doors open by mistake. It was the chance of my life; in I slipped to have a look. He came back for something, saw the very door you've broken standing ajar, and shut it without looking in. So there I was in a nice old trap! I simply daren't call out and give myself away. There was a bit of loose oilcloth on the floor——"

"There is still," said the satellite, pausing in his task.

"I moved the oilcloth, in the end; howked up one end of the board (luckily they weren't groove and tongue), sawed through the next one to it, had it up, too, and got through into the foundations, leaving everything much as I had found it. The place is so small that the oilcloth was obliged to fall in place if it fell anywhere. But I had plenty of time, because my people had gone in to dinner."

"You ought to have been a burglar, sir," said Mr. Drinkwater ironically. "So you covered up a sin with a crime, like half the gentlemen who go through my hands for the first and last time! But how did you get out of the foundations?"

"Oh, that was as easy as pie; I'd often explored them. Do you remember the row I got into, Blanche, for taking you with me once and simply ruining your frock?"

"I remember the frock!" said Blanche.

It was her last contribution to the conversation; immediate developments not only put an end to the further exchange of ancient memories, but rendered it presently impossible by removing Cazalet from the scene with the two detectives. Almost without warning, as in the harlequinade of which they might have been the rascal heroes, all three disappeared down the makeshift trap-door cut by one of them as a schoolboy in his father's floor; and Blanche found herself in sole possession of the stage, a very envious Columbine, indeed!

She hardly even knew how it happened. The satellite must have popped back into the Michelangelo cigar cupboard. He might have called to Mr. Drinkwater, but the only summons that Blanche could remember hearing was almost a sharp one from Drinkwater to Cazalet. A lot of whispering followed in the little place; it was so small that she never saw the hole until it had engulfed two of the trio; the third explorer, Mr. Drinkwater himself, had very courteously turned her out of the library before following the others. And he had said so very little beforehand for her to hear, and so quickly prevented Cazalet from saying anything at all, that she simply could not think what any of them were doing under the floor.

Under her very feet she heard them moving as she waited a bit in the hall; then she left the house by way of the servants' quarters, of course without holding any communication with those mutineers, and only indignant that Mr. Drinkwater should have requested her not to do so.

It was a long half-hour that followed for Blanche Macnair, but she passed it characteristically, and not in morbid probings of the many changes that had come over one young man in less than the course of a summer's day. He was excited at getting back, he had stumbled into a still more exciting situation, so no wonder he was one thing one moment and another the next. That was all that Blanche allowed herself to think of Sweep Cazalet—just then.

She turned her wholesome mind to dogs, which in some ways she knew better and trusted further than men. She had, of course, a dog of her own, but it happened to be on a visit to the doctor or no doubt it would have been in the way all the afternoon. But there was a dog at Uplands, and as yet she had seen nothing of him; he lived in a large kennel in the yard, for he was a large dog and rather friendless. But Blanche knew him by sight, and had felt always sorry for him.

The large kennel was just outside the back door, which was at the top of the cellar steps and at the bottom of two or three leading into the scullery; but Blanche, of course, went round by the garden. She found the poor old dog quite disconsolate in a more canine kennel in a corner of the one that was really worthy of the more formidable carnivora. There was every sign of his being treated as the dangerous dog that Blanche, indeed, had heard he was; the outer bars were further protected by wire netting, which stretched like a canopy over the whole cage; but Blanche let herself in with as little hesitation as she proceeded to beard the poor brute in his inner lair. And he never even barked at her; he just lay whimpering with his tearful nose between his two front paws, as though his dead master had not left him to the servants all his life.

Blanche coaxed and petted him until she almost wept herself; then suddenly and without warning the dog showed his worst side. Out he leaped from wooden sanctuary, almost knocking her down, and barking horribly, but not at Blanche. She followed his infuriated eyes; and the back doorway framed a dusty and grimy figure, just climbing into full length on the cellar stairs, which Blanche had some difficulty in identifying with that of Cazalet.

"Well, you really *are* a Sweep!" she cried when she had slipped out just in time, and the now savage dog was still butting and clawing at his bars. "How did you come out, and where are the enemy?"

"The old way," he answered. "I left them down there."

"And what did you find?"

"I'll tell you later. I can't hear my voice for that infernal dog."

The dreadful barking followed them out of the yard, and round to the right, past the tradesmen's door, to the verge of the drive. Here they met an elderly man in a tremendous hurry—an unstable dotard who instantly abandoned whatever purpose he had formed, and came to anchor in front of them with rheumy eyes and twitching wrinkles.

"Why, if that isn't Miss Blanche!" he quavered. "Do you hear our Roy, miss? I ha'n't heard that go on like that since the night that happened!"

Then Cazalet introduced himself to the old gardener whom he had known all his life; and by rights the man should have wept outright, or else emitted a rustic epigram laden with wise humor. But old Savage hailed from silly Suffolk, and all his life he had belied his surname, but never the alliterative libel on his native country. He took the wanderer's return very much as a matter of course, very much as though he had never been away at all, and was demonstrative only in his further use of the East Anglian pronoun.

"That's a long time since we fared to see you, Mus' Walter," said he; "that's a right long time! And now here's a nice kettle of fish for you to find! But I seen the man, Mus' Walter, and we'll bring that home to him, never you fear!"

"Are you sure that you saw him?" asked Blanche, already under Cazalet's influence on this point.

Savage looked cautiously toward the house before replying; then he lowered his voice dramatically. "Sure, Miss Blanche. Why, I see him that night as plain as I fare to see Mus' Walter now!"

"I should have thought it was too dark to see anybody properly," said Blanche, and Cazalet nodded vigorously to himself.

"Dark, Miss Blanche? Why, that was broad daylight, and if that wasn't there were the lodge lights on to see him by!" His stage voice fell a sepulchral semitone. "But I see him again at the station this very afternoon, I did! I promised not to talk about that—you'll keep that a secret if I tell 'e somethin'?—but I picked him out of half a dozen at the first time of askin'!"

Savage said this with a pleased and vacuous grin, looking Cazalet full in the face; his rheumy eyes were red as the sunset they faced; and Cazalet drew a deep breath as Blanche and he turned back toward the river.

"First time of prompting, I expect!" he whispered. "But there's hope if Savage is their strongest witness."

"Only listen to that dog," said Blanche, as they passed the yard.

# VIII
# FINGER-PRINTS

Hilton Toye was the kind of American who knew London as well as most Londoners, and some other capitals a good deal better than their respective citizens of corresponding intelligence. His travels were mysteriously but enviably interwoven with business; he had an air of enjoying himself, and at the same time making money to pay for his enjoyment, wherever he went. His hotel days were much the same all over Europe: many appointments, but abundant leisure. As, however, he never spoke about his own affairs unless they were also those of the listener—and not always then—half his acquaintances had no idea how he made his money, and the other half wondered how he spent his time. Of his mere interests, which were many, Toye made no such secret; but it was quite impossible to deduce a main industry from the by-products of his level-headed versatility.

Criminology, for example, was an obvious by-product; it was no morbid taste in Hilton Toye, but a scientific hobby that appealed to his mental subtlety. And subtle he was, yet with strange simplicities; grave and dignified, yet addicted to the expressive phraseology of his less enlightened countrymen; naturally sincere, and yet always capable of some ingenuous duplicity.

The appeal of a Blanche Macnair to such a soul needs no analysis. She had struck through all complexities to the core, such as it was or as she might make it. As yet she could only admire the character the man had shown, though it had upset her none the less. At Engelberg he had proposed to her "inside of two weeks," as he had admitted without compunction at the time. It had taken him, he said, about two minutes to make up his mind; but the following summer he had laid more deliberate siege, in accordance with some old idea that she had let fall to soften her first refusal. The result had been the same, only more explicit on both sides. She had denied him the least particle of hope, and he had warned her that she had not heard the last of him by any means, and never would till she married another man. This had incensed her at the time, but a great deal less on subsequent reflection; and such was the position between that pair when Toye and Cazalet landed in England from the same steamer.

On this second day ashore, as Cazalet sat over a late breakfast in Jermyn Street, Toye sent in his card and was permitted to follow it, rather to his surprise. He found his man frankly divided between kidneys-and-bacon and the morning paper, but in a hearty mood, indicative of amends for his great heat in yesterday's argument. A plainer indication was the downright yet sunny manner in which Cazalet at once returned to the contentious topic.

"Well, my dear Toye, what do you think of it now?"

**"What do you think of it now?"**

"I was going to ask you what you thought, but I guess I can see from your face."

"I think the police are rotters for not setting him free last night!"

"Scruton?"

"Yes. Of course, the case'll break down when it comes on next week, but they oughtn't to wait for that. They've no right to detain a man in custody when the bottom's out of their case already."

"But—but the papers claim they've found the very things they were searching for." Toye looked nonplused, as well he might, by an apparently perverse jubilation over such intelligence.

"They haven't found the missing cap!" crowed Cazalet. "What they have found is Craven's watch and keys, and the silver-mounted truncheon that killed him. But they found them in a place where they couldn't possibly have been put by the man identified as Scruton!"

"Say, where was that?" asked Toye with great interest. "My paper only says the things were found, not where."

"No more does mine, but I can tell you, because I helped to find 'em."

"You don't say!"

"You'll never grasp where," continued Cazalet. "In the foundations under the house!"

Details followed in all fulness; the listener might have had a part in the Uplands act of yesterday's drama, might have played in the library scene with his adored Miss Blanche, so vividly was every minute of that crowded hour brought home to him. He also had seen the original writing-cupboard in Michelangelo's old Florentine house; he remembered it perfectly, and said that he could see the replica, with its shelf of a desk stacked with cigars, and the hole in its floor. He was not so sure that he had any very definite conception of the foundations of an English house.

"Ours were like ever so many little tiny rooms," said Cazalet, "where I couldn't stand nearly upright even as a small boy without giving my head a crack against the ground floors. They led into one another by a lot of little manholes—tight fits even for a boy, but nearly fatal to the boss policeman yesterday! I used to get in through one with a door, at the back of a slab in the cellars where they used to keep empty bottles; they keep 'em there still, because that's how I led my party out last night."

Cazalet's little gift of description was not ordered by an equal sense of selection. Hilton Toye, edging in his word in a pause for a gulp of coffee, said he guessed he visualized—but just where had those missing things been found?

"Three or four compartments from the first one under the library," said Cazalet.

"Did you find them?"

"Well, I kicked against the truncheon, but Drinkwater dug it up. The watch and keys were with it."

"Say, were they buried?"

"Only in the loose rubble and brick-dusty stuff that you get in foundations."

"Say, that's bad! That murderer must have known something, or else it's a bully fluke in his favor."

"I don't follow you, Toye."

"I'm thinking of finger-prints. If he'd just've laid those things right down, he'd have left the print of his hand as large as life for Scotland Yard."

"The devil he would!" exclaimed Cazalet. "I wish you'd explain," he added; "remember I'm a wild man from the woods, and only know of these things by the vaguest kind of hearsay and stray paragraphs in the papers. I never knew you could leave your mark so easily as all that."

Toye took the breakfast menu and placed it face downward on the tablecloth. "Lay your hand on that, palm down," he said, "and don't move it for a minute."

Cazalet looked at him a moment before complying; then his fine, shapely, sunburnt hand lay still as plaster under their eyes until Toye told him he might take it up. Of course there was no mark whatever, and Cazalet laughed.

"You should have caught me when I came up from those foundations, not fresh from my tub!" said he.

"You wait," replied Hilton Toye, taking the menu gingerly by the edge, and putting it out of harm's way in the empty toast-rack. "You can't see anything now, but if you come round to the Savoy I'll show you something."

"What?"

"Your prints, sir! I don't say I'm Scotland Yard at the game, but I can do it well enough to show you how it's done. You haven't left your mark upon the paper, but I guess you've left the sweat of your hand; if I snow a little French chalk over it, the chalk'll stick where your hand did, and blow off easily everywhere else. The rest's as simple as all big things. It's hanged a few folks already, but I judge it doesn't have much chance with things that have lain buried in brick-dust. Say, come round to lunch and I'll have your prints ready for you. I'd like awfully to show you how it's done. It would really be a great pleasure."

Cazalet excused himself with decision. He had a full morning in front of him.

He was going to see Miss Macnair's brother, son of the late head of his father's old firm of solicitors, and now one of the partners, to get them either to take up Scruton's case themselves, or else to recommend a firm perhaps more accustomed to criminal practise. Cazalet was always apt to be elaborate in the first person singular, either in the past or in the future tense; but he was more so than usual in explaining his considered intentions in this matter that lay so very near his heart.

"Going to see Scruton, too?" said Toye.

"Not necessarily," was the short reply. But it also was elaborated by Cazalet on a moment's consideration. The fact was that he wanted first to know if it were not possible, by the intervention of a really influential lawyer, to obtain the prisoner's immediate release, at any rate on bail. If impossible, he might hesitate to force himself on Scruton in the prison, but he would see.

"It's a perfect scandal that he should be there at all," said Cazalet, as he rose first and ushered Toye out into the lounge. "Only think: our old gardener saw him run out of the drive at half past seven, when the gong went, when the real murderer must have been shivering in the Michelangelo cupboard, wondering how the devil he was ever going to get out again."

"Then you think old man Craven—begging his poor pardon—was getting out some cigars when the man, whoever he was, came in and knocked him on the head?"

Cazalet nodded vigorously. "That's the likeliest thing of all!" he cried. "Then the gong went—there may even have come a knock at the door—and there was that cupboard standing open at his elbow."

"With a hole in the floor that might have been made for him?"

"As it happens, yes; he'd search every inch like a rat in a trap, you see; and there it was as I'd left it twenty years before."

"Well, it's a wonderful yarn!" exclaimed Hilton Toye, and he lighted the cigar that Cazalet had given him.

"I think it may be thought one if the police ever own how they made their find," agreed Cazalet, laughing and looking at his watch. Toye had never heard him laugh so often. "By the way, Drinkwater doesn't want any of all this to come out until he's dragged his man before the beak again."

"Which you mean to prevent?"

"If only I can! I more or less promised not to talk, however, and I'm sure you won't. You knew so much already, you may just as well know the rest this week as well as next, if you don't mind keeping it to yourself."

45

Nobody could have minded this particular embargo less than Hilton Toye; and in nothing was he less like Cazalet, who even now had the half-regretful and self-excusing air of the impulsive person who has talked too freely and discovered it too late. But he had been perfectly delightful to Hilton Toye, almost too appreciative, if anything, and now very anxious to give him a lift in his taxi. Toye, however, had shopping to do in the very street that they were in, and he saw Cazalet off with a smile that was as yet merely puzzled, and not unfriendly until he had time to recall Miss Blanche's part in the strange affair of the previous afternoon.

Say, weren't they rather intimate, those two, even if they had known each other all their lives? He had it from Blanche (with her second refusal) that she was not, and never had been, engaged. And a fellow who only wrote to her once in a year—still, they must have been darned intimate, and this funny affair would bring them together again quicker than anything.

Say, what a funny affair it was when you came to think of it! Funny all through, it now struck Toye; beginning on board ship with that dream of Cazalet's about the murdered man, leading to all that talk of the old grievance against him, and culminating in his actually finding the implements of the crime in his inspired efforts to save the man of whose innocence he was so positive. Say, if that Cazalet had not been on his way home from Australia at the time!

Like many deliberate speakers, Toye thought like lightning, and had reached this point before he was a hundred yards from the hotel; then he thought of something else, and retraced his steps. He retraced them even to the table at which he had sat with Cazalet not very many minutes ago; the waiter was only now beginning to clear away.

"Say, waiter, what have you done with the menu that was in that toast-rack? There was something on it that we rather wanted to keep."

"I thought there was, sir," said the English waiter at that admirable hotel. Toye, however, prepared to talk to him like an American uncle of Dutch extraction.

"You thought that, and you took it away?"

"Not at all, sir. I 'appened to observe the other gentleman put the menu in his pocket, behind your back as you were getting up, because I passed a remark about it to the head waiter at the time!"

# IX
# FAIR WARNING

It was much more than a map of the metropolis that Toye carried in his able head. He knew the right places for the right things, from his tailor's at one end of Jermyn Street to his hatter's at the other, and from the man for collars and dress shirts, in another of St. James', to the only man for soft shirts, on Piccadilly. Hilton Toye visited them all in turn this fine September morning, and found the select team agreeably disengaged, readier than ever to suit him. Then he gazed critically at his boots. He was not so dead sure that he had struck the only man for boots. There had been a young fellow aboard the *Kaiser Fritz*, quite a little bit of a military blood, who had come ashore in a pair of cloth tops that had rather unsettled Mr. Toye's mind just on that one point.

He thought of this young fellow when he was through with the soft-shirt man on Piccadilly. They had diced for a drink or two in the smoking-room, and Captain Aylmer had said he would like to have Toye see his club any time he was passing and cared to look in for lunch. He had said so as though he would like it a great deal, and suddenly Toye had a mind to take him at his word right now. The idea began with those boots with cloth tops, but that was not all there was to it; there was something else that had been at the back of Toye's mind all morning, and now took charge in front.

Aylmer had talked some about a job in the war office that enabled him to lunch daily at the Rag; but what his job had been aboard a German steamer Toye did not know and was not the man to inquire. It was no business of his, anyway. Reference to a card, traded for his own in Southampton Water, and duly filed in his cigarette-case, reminded him of the Rag's proper style and title. And there he was eventually entertained to a sound, workmanlike, rather expeditious meal.

"Say, did you see the cemetery at Genoa?" suddenly inquired the visitor on their way back through the hall. A martial bust had been admired extravagantly before the question.

"Never want to see it again, or Genoa either," said Captain Aylmer. "The smoking-room's this way."

"I judge you didn't care a lot about the city?" pursued Toye as they found a corner.

"Genoa? Oh, I liked it all right, but you get fed up in a couple of days neither

47

ashore nor afloat. It's a bit amphibious. Of course you can go to a hotel, if you like; but not if you're only a poor British soldier."

"Did you say you were there two days?" Toye was cutting his cigar as though it were a corn.

"Two whole days, and we'd had a night in the Bay of Naples just before."

"Is that so? I only came aboard at Genoa. I guess I was wise," added Toye, as though he was thinking of something else. There was no sort of feeling in his voice, but he was sucking his left thumb.

"I say, you've cut yourself!"

"I guess it's nothing. Knife too sharp; please don't worry, Captain Aylmer. I was going to say I only got on at Genoa, and they couldn't give me a room to myself. I had to go in with Cazalet; that's how I saw so much of him."

It was Toye's third separate and independent attempt to introduce the name and fame of Cazalet as a natural topic of conversation. Twice his host had listened with adamantine politeness; this time he was enjoying quite the second-best liqueur brandy to be had at the Rag; and he leaned back in his chair.

"You were rather impressed with him, weren't you?" said Captain Aylmer. "Well, frankly, I wasn't, but it may have been my fault. It does rather warp one's judgment to be shot out to Aden on a potty job at this time o' year."

So that was where he had been? Yes, and by Jove he had to see a man about it all at three o'clock.

"One of the nuts," explained Captain Aylmer, keeping his chair with fine restraint. Toye rose with finer alacrity. "I hope you won't think me rude," said the captain, "but I'm afraid I really mustn't keep him waiting."

Toye said the proper things all the way to the hat-stand, and there took frontal measures as a last resort. "I was only going to ask you one thing about Mr. Cazalet," he said, "and I guess I've a reason for asking, though there's no time to state it now. What did you think of him, Captain Aylmer, on the whole?"

"Ah, there you have me. 'On the whole' is just the difficulty," said Aylmer, answering the straight question readily enough. "I thought he was a very good chap as far as Naples, but after Genoa he was another being. I've sometimes wondered what happened in his three or four days ashore."

"Three or *four*, did you say?"

And at the last moment Toye would have played Wedding Guest to Aylmer's Ancient Mariner.

"Yes; you see, he knew these German boats waste a couple of days at Genoa, so he landed at Naples and did his Italy overland. Rather a good idea, I thought, especially as he said he had friends in Rome; but we never heard of 'em beforehand, and I should have let the whole thing strike me a bit sooner if I'd been Cazalet. Soon enough to take a hand-bag and a tooth-brush, eh? And I don't think I should have run it quite so fine at Genoa, either. But there are rum birds in this world, and always will be!"

Toye felt one himself as he picked his way through St. James' Square. If it had not been just after lunch, he would have gone straight and had a cocktail, for of course he knew the only place for *them*. What he did was to slue round out of the square, and to obtain for the asking, at another old haunt, on Cockspur Street, the latest little time-table of continental trains. This he carried, not on foot but in a taxi, to the Savoy Hotel, where it kept him busy in his own room for the best part of another hour. But by that time Hilton Toye looked more than an hour older than on sitting down at his writing-table with pencil, paper and the little book of trains; he looked horrified, he looked distressed, and yet he looked crafty, determined and immensely alive. He proceeded, however, to take some of the life out of himself, and to add still more to his apparent age, by repairing for more inward light and leading to a Turkish bath.

Now the only Turkish bath, according to Hilton Toye's somewhat exclusive code, was not even a hundred yards from Cazalet's hotel; and there the visitor of the morning again presented himself before the afternoon; now merely a little worn, as a man will look after losing a stone an hour on a warm afternoon, and a bit blue again about the chin, which of course looked a little deeper and stronger on that account.

Cazalet was not in; his friend would wait, and in fact waited over an hour in the little lounge. An evening paper was offered to him; he took it listlessly, scarcely looked at it at first, then tore it in his anxiety to find something he had quite forgotten—from the newspaper end. But he was waiting as stoically as before when Cazalet arrived in tremendous spirits.

"Stop and dine!" he cried out at once.

"Sorry I can't; got to go and see somebody," said Hilton Toye.

"Then you must have a drink."

"No, I thank you," said Toye, with the decisive courtesy of a total abstainer.

"You look as if you wanted one; you don't look a bit fit," said Cazalet most kindly.

"Nor am I, sir!" exclaimed Toye. "I guess London's no place for me in the

49

fall. Just as well, too, I judge, since I've got to light out again straight away."

"You haven't!"

"Yes, sir, this very night. That's the worst of a business that takes you to all the capitals of Europe in turn. It takes you so long to flit around that you never know when you've got to start in again."

"Which capital is it this time?" said Cazalet. His exuberant geniality had been dashed very visibly for the moment. But already his high spirits were reasserting themselves; indeed, a cynic with an ear might have caught the note of sudden consolation in the question that Cazalet asked so briskly.

"Got to go down to Rome," said Toye, watching the effect of his words.

"But you've just come back from there!" Cazalet looked no worse than puzzled.

"No, sir, I missed Rome out; that was my mistake, and here's this situation been developing behind my back."

"What situation?"

"Oh, why, it wouldn't interest you! But I've got to go down to Rome, whether I like it or not, and I don't like it any, because I don't have any friends there. And that's what I'm doing right here. I was wondering if you'd do something for me, Cazalet?"

"If I can," said Cazalet, "with pleasure." But his smiles were gone.

"I was wondering if you'd give me an introduction to those friends of yours in Rome!"

There was a little pause, and Cazalet's tongue just showed between his lips, moistening them. It was at that moment the only touch of color in his face.

"*Did* I tell you I'd any friends there?"

The sound of his voice was perhaps less hoarse than puzzled. Toye made himself chuckle as he sat looking up out of somber eyes.

"Well, if you didn't," said he, "I guess I must have dreamed it!"

———————————

50

# X
# THE WEEK OF THEIR LIVES

"Toye's gone back to Italy," said Cazalet. "He says he may be away only a week. Let's make it the week of our lives!"

The scene was the little room it pleased Blanche to call her parlor, and the time a preposterously early hour of the following forenoon. Cazalet might have 'planed down from the skies into her sunny snuggery, though his brand-new Burberry rather suggested another extravagant taxicab. But Blanche saw only his worn excited face; and her own was not at its best in her sheer amazement.

If she had heard the last two sentences, to understand them at the time she would have felt bound to take them up first, and to ask how on earth Mr. Toye could affect her plans or pleasures. But such was the effect of the preceding statement that all the rest was several moments on the way to her comprehension, where it arrived, indeed, more incomprehensible than ever, but not worth making a fuss about then.

"Italy!" she had ejaculated meanwhile. "*When* did he go?"

"Nine o'clock last night."

"But"—she checked herself—"I simply can't understand it, that's all!"

"Why? Have you seen him since the other afternoon?"

His manner might have explained those other two remarks, now bothering her when it was too late to notice them; on the other hand, she was by no means sure that it did. He might simply dislike Toye, and that again might explain his extraordinary heat over the argument at Littleford. Blanche began to feel the air somewhat heavily charged with explanations, either demanded or desired; they were things she hated, and she determined not to add to them if she could help it.

"I haven't set eyes on him again," she said. "But he's been seen here—in a taxi."

"Who saw him?"

"Martha—if she's not mistaken."

This was a little disingenuous, as will appear; but that impetuous Sweep was in a merciful hurry to know something else.

"When was this, Blanche?"

"Just about dark—say seven or so. She owns it was about dark," said Blanche, though she felt ashamed of herself.

"Well, it's just possible. He left me about six; said he had to see some one, too, now I think of it. But I'd give a bit to know what he was doing, messing about down here at the last moment!"

Blanche liked this as little as anything that Cazalet had said yet, and he had said nothing that she did like this morning. But there were allowances to be made for him, she knew. And yet to strengthen her knowledge, or rather to let him confirm it for her, either by word or by his silence, she stated a certain case for him aloud.

"Poor old Sweep!" she laughed. "It's a shame that you should have come home to be worried like this."

"I am worried," he said simply.

"I think it's just splendid, all you're doing for that poor man, but especially the way you're doing it."

"I wish to God you wouldn't say that, Blanche!"

He paid her the compliment of speaking exactly as he would have spoken to a man; or rather, she happened to be the woman to take it as a compliment.

"But I do say it, Sweep! I've heard all about it from Charlie. He rang me up last night."

"You're on the telephone, are you?"

"Everybody is in these days. Where have you lived? Oh, I forgot!" And she laughed. Anything to lift this duet of theirs out of the minor key!

"But what does old Charlie really think of the case? That's more to the point," said Cazalet uneasily.

"Well, he seemed to fear there was no chance of bail before the adjourned hearing. But I rather gathered he was not going to be in it himself?"

"No. We decided on one of those sportsmen who love rushing in where a family lawyer like Charlie owns to looking down his nose. I've seen the chap, and primed him up about old Savage, and our find in the foundations. He says he'll make an example of Drinkwater, and Charlie says they call him the Bobby's Bugbear!"

"But surely he'll have to tell his client who's behind him?"

"No. He's just the type who would have rushed in, anyhow. And it'll be time enough to put Scruton under obligations when I've got him off!"

Blanche looked at the troubled eyes avoiding hers, and thought that she had never heard of a fine thing being done so finely. This very shamefacedness appealed to her intensely, and yet last night Charlie had said that old Sweep was in such tremendous spirits about it all! Why was he so down this morning?

She only knew she could have taken his hand, but for a very good reason why she could not. She had even to guard against an equivocally sympathetic voice or manner, as she asked, "How long did they remand him for?"

"Eight days."

"Well, then, you'll know the best or the worst to-day week!"

"Yes!" he said eagerly, almost himself again. "But, whichever way it goes, I'm afraid it means trouble for me, Blanche; some time or other I'll tell you why; but that's why I want this to be the week of our lives."

So he really meant what he had said before. The phrase had been no careless misuse of words; but neither, after all, did it necessarily apply to Mr. Toye. That was something. It made it easier for Blanche not to ask questions.

Cazalet had gone out on the balcony; now he called to her; and there was no taxi, but a smart open car, waiting in the road, its brasses blazing in the sun, an immaculate chauffeur at the wheel.

"Whose is that, Sweep?"

"Mine, for the week I'm talking about! I mean ours, if you'd only buck up and get ready to come out! A week doesn't last forever, you know!"

Blanche ran off to Martha, who fussed and hindered her with the best intentions. It would have been difficult to say which was the more excited of the two. But the old nurse would waste time in perfectly fatuous reminiscences of the very earliest expeditions in which Mr. Cazalet had lead and Blanche had followed, and what a bonny pair they had made even then, etc. Severely snubbed on that subject, she took to peering at her mistress, once her bairn, with furtive eagerness and impatience; for Blanche, on her side, looked as though she had something on her mind, and, indeed, had made one or two attempts to get it off. She had to force it even in the end.

"There's just one thing I want to say before I go, Martha."

"Yes, dearie, yes?"

"You know when Mr. Toye called yesterday, and I was out?"

"Oh, Mr. Toye; yes, I remember, Miss Blanche."

"Well, I don't want you to say that he came in and waited half an hour in vain; in fact, not that he came in at all, or that you're even sure you saw him, unless, of course, you're asked."

"Who should ask me, I wonder?"

"Well, I don't know, but there seems to be a little bad blood between Mr. Toye and Mr. Cazalet."

Martha looked for a moment as though she were about to weep, and then for another moment as though she would die of laughing. But a third moment she celebrated by making an utter old fool of herself, as she would have been told to her face by anybody but Blanche, whose yellow hair was being disarranged by the very hands that had helped to imprison it under that motor-hat and veil.

"Oh, Blanchie, is that all you have to tell me?" said Martha.

And then the week of their lives began.

———————————

# XI
# IN COUNTRY AND IN TOWN

The weather was true to them, and this was a larger matter than it might have been. They were not making love. They were "not out for that," as Blanche herself actually told Martha, with annihilating scorn, when the old dear looked both knowing and longing-to-know at the end of the first day's run. They were out to enjoy themselves, and that seemed shocking to Martha "unless something was coming of it." She had just sense enough to keep her conditional clause to herself.

Yet if they were only out to enjoy themselves, in the way Miss Blanche vowed and declared (more shame for her), they certainly had done wonders for a start. Martha could hardly credit all they said they had done, and as an embittered pedestrian there was nothing that she would "put past" one of those nasty motors. It said very little for Mr. Cazalet, by the way, in Martha's private opinion, that he should take her Miss Blanche out in a car at all; if he had turned out as well as she had hoped, and "meant anything," a nice boat on the river would have been better for them both than all that tearing through the air in a cloud of smoky dust; it would also have been much less expensive, and far more "the thing".

But, there, to see and hear the child after the first day! She looked so bonny that for a time Martha really believed that Mr. Cazalet had "spoken," and allowed herself to admire him also as he drove off later with his wicked lamps alight. But Blanche would only go on and on about her day, the glories of the Ripley Road and the grandeur of Hindhead. She had brought back heaps of heather and bunches of leaves just beginning to turn; they were all over the little house before Cazalet had been gone ten minutes. But Blanche hadn't forgotten her poor old Martha; she was not one to forget people, especially when she loved and yet had to snub them. Martha's portion was picture post-cards of the Gibbet and other landmarks of the day.

"And if you're good," said Blanche, "you shall have some every day, and an album to keep them in forever and ever. And won't that be nice when it's all over, and Mr. Cazalet's gone back to Australia?"

Crueller anticlimax was never planned, but Martha's face had brought it on her; and now it remained to make her see for herself what an incomparably good time they were having so far.

"It was a simply splendid lunch at the Beacon, and *such* a tea at Byfleet, coming back another way," explained Blanche, who was notoriously indifferent about her food, but also as a rule much hungrier than she seemed to-night. "It must be that tea, my dear. It was *too* much. To-morrow I'm to take the *Sirram*, and I want Walter to see if he can't get a billy and show me how they make tea in the bush; but he says it simply couldn't be done without methylated."

The next day they went over the Hog's Back, and the next day right through London into Hertfordshire. This was a tremendous experience. The car was a good one from a good firm, and the chauffeur drove like an angel through the traffic, so that the teeming city opened before them from end to end. Then the Hertfordshire hedges and meadows and timber were the very things after the Hog's Back and Hindhead; not so wonderful, of course, but more like old England and less like the bush; and before the day was out they had seen, through dodging London on the way back, the Harrow boys like a lot of young butlers who had changed hats with the maids, and Eton boys as closely resembling a convocation of slack curates.

Then there was their Buckinghamshire day—Chalfont St. Giles and Hughenden—and almost detached experiences such as the churchyard at Stoke Poges, where Cazalet repeated astounding chunks of its *Elegy*, learned as long ago as his preparatory school-days, and the terrible disillusion of Hounslow Heath and its murderous trams.

Then there was the wood they found where gipsies had been camping, where they resolved that moment to do the same, just exactly in every detail as Cazalet had so often done it in the bush; so that flesh and flour were fetched from the neighboring village, and he sat on his heels and turned them into mutton and damper in about a minute; and after that a real camp-fire till long after dark, and a shadowy chauffeur smoking his pipe somewhere in the other shadows, and thinking them, of course, quite mad. The critic on the hearth at home thought even worse of them than that. But Blanche only told the truth when she declared that the whole thing had been her idea; and she might have added, a bitter disappointment to her, because Walter simply would not talk about the bush itself, and never had since that first hour in the old empty schoolroom at Littleford.

(By the way, she had taken to calling him Walter to his face.)

Of other conversation, however, there was not and never had been the slightest dearth between them; but it was, perhaps, a sad case of quantity. These were two outdoor souls, and the one with the interesting life no longer spoke about it. Neither was a great reader, even of the papers, though Blanche liked poetry as she liked going to church; but each had the mind that could batten quite amiably on other people. So there was a deal of talk about neighbors down the river, and some of it was scandal, and all was gossip; and there was a great deal about what Blanche called their stone-age days, but again far less about themselves when young than there had been at Littleford, that first day. And so much for their conversation, once for all; it was frankly that of two very ordinary persons, placed in an extraordinary position to which they had shut their eyes for a week.

They must have had between them, however, some rudimentary sense of construction; for their final fling, if not just the most inspiring, was at least unlike all the rest. It was almost as new to Blanche, and now much more so to Cazalet; it appealed as strongly to their common stock of freshness and simplicity. Yet cause and effect were alike undeniably lacking in distinction. It began with cartloads of new clothes from Cazalet's old tailor, and it ended in a theater and the Carlton.

Martha surpassed herself, of course; she had gone about for days (or rather mornings and evenings) in an aggressive silence, her lips provocatively pursed; but now the time had come for her to speak out, and that she did. If Miss Blanche had no respect for herself, there were those who had some for her, just as there were others who seemed to have forgotten the meaning of the word. The euphemistic plural disappeared at the first syllable from Blanche. It was nothing to Martha that she had been offered a place in the car (beside that forward young man) more days than one; well did Mr. Cazalet know her feelings about motors before he made her the offer. But she was not saying anything about what was past. *This* was the limit; an expression which only sullied Martha's lips because Blanche had just applied it to her interference. It was not behaving as a gentleman; it was enough to work unpleasant miracles in her poor parents' graves; and though Martha herself would die sooner than inform Mr. Charlie or the married sisters, other people were beginning to talk, and when this came out she knew who would get the blame.

So Blanche seemed rather flushed and very spirited at the short and early dinner at Dieudonne's; but it was a fact that the motoring had affected her skin, besides making her eyes look as though she had been doing what she simply never did. It had also toned up the lower part of Cazalet's face to match the rest; otherwise he was more like a meerschaum pipe than ever, with the white frieze across his forehead (but now nothing else) to stamp him from the wilds. And soon nobody was laughing louder at Mr. Payne and Mr. Grossmith; nobody looked better qualified for his gaiety stall, nobody less like a predestined figure in impending melodrama.

So also at the Carlton later; more champagne, of course, and the jokes of the evening to replenish a dwindling store, and the people at the other tables to give a fresh fillip to the game of gossip. Blanche looked as well as any of them in a fresher way than most, and Cazalet a noble creature in all his brand-new glory; and she winced with pride at the huge tip she saw him give the waiter; for an old friend may be proud of an old friend, surely! Then they got a good place for watching more people in the lounge; and the fiddling conductor proved the best worth watching of the lot, and was pronounced the very best performer that Cazalet had ever heard in all his life. Many other items were praised in the same fervent formula, which Blanche confirmed about everything except his brandy and cigar.

Above all was it delightful to feel that their beloved car was waiting for them outside, to whirl them out of all this racket just as late as they liked; for quite early in the week (and this was a glaring aggravation in Martha's eyes) Cazalet had taken lodgings for himself and driver in those very Nell Gwynne Cottages where Hilton Toye had stayed before him.

All the evening nothing had been better of its kind than this music at the very end; and, of course, it was the kind for Blanche and Cazalet, who for his part liked anything with a tune, but could never remember one to save his life. Yet when they played an aged waltz, actually in its second decade, just upon half past twelve, even Cazalet cocked his head and frowned, as though he had heard the thing before.

"I seem to know that," he said. "I believe I've danced to it."

"I have," said Blanche. "Often," she added suddenly; and then, "I suppose you sometimes dance in the bush, Walter?"

"Sometimes."

"That's where it was, then."

"I don't think so. You couldn't get that tremendous long note on a piano. There it goes again—bars and bars of it! That's what I seem to remember."

Blanche's face never changed. "Now, that's the end. They're beginning to put the lights out, Walter. Don't you think we'd better go?"

# XII
# THE THOUSANDTH MAN

It had been new life to them, but now it was all over. It was the last evening of their week, and they were spending it rather silently on Blanche's balcony.

"I make it at least three hundred," said Cazalet, and knocked out a pipe that might have been a gag. "You see, we were very seldom under fifty!"

"Speak for yourself, please! My longevity's a tender point," said Blanche, who looked as though she had no business to have her hair up, as she sat in a pale cross-fire between a lamp-post and her lighted room.

Cazalet protested that he had only meant their mileage in the car; he made himself extremely intelligible now, as he often would when she rallied him in a serious voice. Evidently that was not the way to rouse him up to-night, and she wanted to cheer him after all that he had done for her. Better perhaps not to burke the matter that she knew was on his mind.

"Well, it's been a heavenly time," she assured him just once more. "And to-morrow it's pretty sure to come all right about Scruton, isn't it?"

"Yes! To-morrow we shall probably have Toye back," he answered with grim inconsequence.

"What has that to do with it, Walter?"

"Oh, nothing, of course."

But still his tone was grim and heavy, with a schoolboy irony that he would not explain but could not keep to himself. So Mr. Toye must be turned out of the conversation, though it was not Blanche who had dragged him in. She wished people would stick to their point. She meant to make people, just for once and for their own good; but it took time to find so many fresh openings, and he only cutting up another pipeful of that really rather objectionable bush tobacco.

"There's one thing I've rather wanted to ask you," she began.

"Yes?" said Cazalet.

"You said the other day that it would mean worry for you in any case—after to-morrow—whether the charge is dismissed or not!"

His wicker chair creaked under him.

"I don't see why it should," she persisted, "if the case falls through."

"Well, that's where I come in," he had to say.

"Surely you mean just the other way about? If they commit the man for trial, then you do come in, I know. It's like your goodness."

"I wish you wouldn't say that! It hurts me!"

"Then will you explain yourself? It's not fair to tell me so much, and then to leave out just the bit that's making you miserable!"

The trusty, sisterly, sensible voice, half bantering but altogether kind, genuinely interested if the least bit inquisitive, too, would have gone to a harder or more hardened heart than beat on Blanche's balcony that night. Yet as Cazalet lighted his pipe he looked old enough to be her father.

"I'll tell you some time," he puffed.

"It's only a case of two heads," said Blanche. "I know you're bothered, and I should like to help, that's all."

"You couldn't."

"How do you know? I believe you're going to devote yourself to this poor man—if you can get him off—I mean, when you do."

"Well?" he said.

"Surely I could help you there! Especially if he's ill," cried Blanche, encouraged by his silence. "I'm not half a bad nurse, really!"

"I'm certain you're not."

"Does he *look* very ill?"

She had been trying to avoid the direct question as far as possible, but this one seemed so harmless. Yet it was received in a stony silence unlike any that had gone before. It was as though Cazalet neither moved nor breathed, whereas he had been all sighs and fidgets just before. His pipe was out already—that was the one merit of bush tobacco, it required constant attention—and he did not look like lighting it again.

Until to-night they had not mentioned Scruton since the motoring began. That had been a tacit rule of the road, of wayside talk and indoor orgy. But Blanche had always assumed that Cazalet had been to see him in the prison; and now he told her that he never had.

"I can't face him," he cried under his breath, "and that's the truth! Let me get him out of this hole, and I'm his man forever; but until I do, while there's a chance of failing, I simply can't face the fellow. It isn't as if he'd asked to see me. Why should I force myself upon him?"

"He hasn't asked to see you because he doesn't know what you're doing for him!" Blanche leaned forward as eagerly as she was speaking, all her repressed feelings coming to their own in her for just a moment. "He doesn't know because I do believe you wouldn't have him told that you'd arrived, lest he should suspect! You *are* a brick, Sweep, you really are!"

He was too much of one to sit still under the name. He sprang up, beating his hands. "Why shouldn't I be—to him—to a poor devil who's been through all he's been through? Ten years! Just think of it; no, it's unthinkable to you or me. And it all started in our office; we were to blame for not keeping our eyes open; things couldn't have come to such a pass if we'd done our part, my poor old father for one—I can't help saying it—and I myself for another. Talk about contributory negligence! We were negligent, as well as blind. We didn't know a villain when we saw one, and we let him make another villain under our noses; and the second one was the only one we could see in his true colors, even then. Do you think we owe him nothing now? Don't you think *I* owe him something, as the only man left to pay?"

But Blanche made no attempt to answer his passionate questions. He had let himself go at last; it relieved her also in a way, for it was the natural man back again on her balcony. But he had set Blanche off thinking on other lines than he intended.

"I'm thinking of what *he* must have felt he owed Mr. Craven and—and Ethel!" she owned.

"I don't bother my head over either of them," returned Cazalet harshly. "He was never a white man in his lifetime, and she was every inch his daughter. Scruton's the one I pity—because—because I've suffered so much from that man myself."

"But you don't think he did it!" Blanche was sharp enough to interrupt.

"No—no—but if he had!"

"You'd still stand by him?"

"I've told you so before. I meant to take him back to Australia with me—I never told you that—but I meant to take him, and not a soul out there to know who he was." He sighed aloud over the tragic stopper on that plan.

"And would you still?" she asked.

"If I could get him off."

"Guilty or not guilty?"

"Rather!"

There was neither shame, pose, nor hesitation about that. Blanche went through into the room without a word, but her eyes shone finely in the lamplight. Then she returned with a book, and stood half in the balcony, framed as in a panel, looking for a place.

"You remind me of *The Thousandth Man*," she told him as she found it.

"Who was he?"

"He's every man who does a thousandth part of what you're doing!" said Blanche with confidence. And then she read, rather shyly and not too well:

"'One man in a thousand, Solomon says,

   Will stick more close than a brother.

And it's worth while seeking him half your days

   If you find him before the other.

Nine hundred and ninety-nine depend

   On what the world sees in you,

But the Thousandth Man will stand your friend

   With the whole round world agin you.'"

"I should hope he would," said Cazalet, "if he's a man at all."

"But this is the bit for you," said Blanche:

"'His wrong's your wrong, and his right's your right,

   In season or out of season.

Stand up and back it in all men's sight—

   With *that* for your only reason!

Nine hundred and ninety-nine can't bide

   The shame or mocking or laughter,

But the Thousandth Man will stand by your side

   *To the gallows-foot—and after!*'"

The last italics were in Blanche's voice, and it trembled, but so did Cazalet's as he cried out in his formula:

"That's the finest thing I ever heard in all my life! But it's true, and so it should be. *I* don't take any credit for it."

"Then you're all the more the thousandth man!"

He caught her suddenly by the shoulders. His rough hands trembled; his jaw worked. "Look here, Blanchie! If *you* had a friend, wouldn't you do the same?"

"Yes, if I'd such a friend as all that," she faltered.

"You'd stand by his side 'to the gallows-foot'—if he was swine enough to let you?"

"I dare say I might."

"However bad a thing it was—murder, if you like—and however much he was mixed up in it—not like poor Scruton?"

"I'd try to stick to him," she said simply.

"Then you're the thousandth woman," said Cazalet. "God bless you, Blanchie!"

**"God bless you, Blanchie!"**

He turned on his heel in the balcony, and a minute later found the room behind him empty. He entered, stood thinking, and suddenly began looking all over for the photograph of himself, with a beard, which he had seen there a week before.

# XIII
# QUID PRO QUO

It was his blessing that had done it; up to then she had controlled her feelings in a fashion worthy of the title just bestowed upon her. If only he had stopped at that, and kept his blessing to himself! It sounded so very much more like a knell that Blanche had begun first to laugh, and then to make such a fool of herself (as she herself reiterated) that she was obliged to run away in the worst possible order.

But that was not the end of those four superfluous words of final benediction; before the night was out they had solved, to Blanche's satisfaction, the hitherto impenetrable mystery of Cazalet's conduct.

He had done something in Australia, something that fixed a gulf between him and her. Blanche did not mean something wrong, much less a crime, least of all any sort of complicity in the great crime which had been committed while he was on his way home. Obviously he could have had no connection with that, until days afterward as the accused man's friend. Yet he had on his conscience some act or other of which he was ashamed to speak. It might even itself be shameful; that was what his whole manner had suggested, but what Blanche was least ready and at the same time least unwilling to believe. She felt she could forgive such an old friend almost anything. But she believed the worst he had done was to emulate his friend Mr. Potts, and to get engaged or perhaps actually married to somebody in the bush.

There was no reason why he should not; there never had been any sort or kind of understanding between herself and him; it was only as lifelong friends that they had written to each other, and that only once a year. Lifelong friendships are traditionally fatal to romance. Blanche could remember only one occasion on which their friendship had risen to something more—or fallen to something less! She knew which it had been to her; especially just afterward, when all his troubles had come and he had gone away without another word of that kind. He had resolved not to let her tie herself, and so had tied her all the tighter, if not tighter still by never stating his resolve. But to go as far as this is to go two or three steps further than Blanche went in her perfectly rational retrospect: she simply saw, as indeed she had always seen, that they had both been free as air; and if he was free no longer, she had absolutely no cause for complaint, even if she was fool enough to feel it.

All this she saw quite clearly in her very honest heart. And yet, he might have told her; he need not have flown to see her, the instant he landed, or seemed so overjoyed, and such a boy again, or made so much of her and their common memories! He need not have begun begging her, in a minute, to go out to Australia, and then never have mentioned it again; he might just as well have told her if he had or hoped to have a wife to welcome her! Of course he saw it afterward, himself; that was why the whole subject of Australia had been dropped so suddenly and for good. Most likely he had married beneath him; if so, she was very sorry, but he might have said that he was married. Had Blanche been analyzing herself, and not just the general position of things, she would have had hereabouts to account to her conscience for a not unpleasing spasm at the sudden thought of his being unhappily married all the time.

One proof was that he had utterly forgotten all about the waltz of *Eldorado*—even its name! No; it had some vague associations for him, and that was worse than none at all. Blanche had its long note (not "bars and bars," though, Sweep) wailing in her head all night. And so for him their friendship had only fallen to something lower, to that hateful haunting tune that he could not even decently forget!

Curiously enough, it was over Martha that she felt least able to forgive him. Martha would say nothing, but her unspoken denunciations of Cazalet would be only less intolerable than her unspoken sympathy with Blanche. Martha had been perfectly awful about the whole thing. And Martha had committed the final outrage of being perfectly right, from her idiotic point of view.

Now among all these meditations of a long night, and of a still longer day, in which nobody even troubled to send her word of the case at Kingston, it would be too much to say that no thought of Hilton Toye ever entered the mind of Blanche. She could not help liking him; he amused her immensely; and he had proposed to her twice, and warned her he would again. She felt the force of his warning, because she felt his force of character and will. She literally felt these forces, as actual emanations from the strongest personality that had ever impinged upon her own. Not only was he strong, but capable and cultivated; and he knew the whole world as most people only knew some hole or corner of it; and could be most interesting without ever talking about himself or other people.

In the day of reaction, such considerations were bound to steal in as single spies, each with a certain consolation, not altogether innocent of comparisons. But the battalion of Toye's virtues only marched on Blanche when Martha came to her, on the little green rug of a lawn behind the house, to say that Mr. Toye himself had called and was in the drawing-room.

Blanche stole up past the door, and quickly made herself smarter than she had ever done by day for Walter Cazalet; at least she put on a "dressy" blouse, her calling skirt (which always looked new), and did what she could to her hair. All this was only because Mr. Toye always came down as if it were Mayfair, and it was rotten to make people feel awkward if you could help it. So in sailed Blanche, in her very best for the light of day, to be followed as soon as possible by the silver teapot, though she had just had tea herself. And there stood Hilton Toye, chin blue and collar black, his trousers all knees and no creases, exactly as he had jumped out of the boat-train.

"I guess I'm not fit to speak to you," he said, "but that's just what I've come to do—for the third time!"

"Oh, Mr. Toye!" cried Blanche, really frightened by the face that made his meaning clear. It relaxed a little as she shrank involuntarily, but the compassion in his eyes and mouth did not lessen their steady determination.

"I didn't have time to make myself presentable," he explained. "I thought you wouldn't have me waste a moment if you understood the situation. I want your promise to marry me right now!"

Blanche began to breathe again. Evidently he was on the eve of yet another of his journeys, probably back to America, and he wanted to go over engaged; at first she had thought he had bad news to break to her, but this was no worse than she had heard before. Only it was more difficult to cope with him; everything was different, and he so much more pressing and precipitate. She had never met this Hilton Toye before. Yes; she was distinctly frightened by him. But in a minute she had ceased to be frightened of herself; she knew her own mind once more, and spoke it much as he had spoken his, quite compassionately, but just as tersely to the point.

"One moment," he interrupted. "I said nothing about my feelings, because they're a kind of stale proposition by this time; but for form's sake I may state there's no change there, except in the only direction I guess a person's feelings are liable to change toward you, Miss Blanche! I'm a worse case than ever, if that makes any difference."

Blanche shook her yellow head. "Nothing can," she said. "There must be no possible mistake about it this time, because I want you to be very good and never ask me again. And I'm glad you didn't make all the proper speeches, because I needn't either, Mr. Toye! But—I know my own mind better than I ever did until this very minute—and I could simply never marry you!"

Toye accepted his fate with a ready resignation, little short of alacrity. There was a gleam in his somber eyes, and his blue chin came up with a jerk. "That's talking!" said he. "Now will you promise me never to marry Cazalet?"

"Mr. Toye!"

"That's talking, too, and I guess I mean it to be. It's not all dog-in-the-manger, either. I want that promise a lot more than I want the other. You needn't marry me, Miss Blanche, but you mustn't marry Cazalet."

Blanche was blazing. "But this is simply outrageous——"

"I claim there's an outrageous cause for it. Are you prepared to swear what I ask, and trust me as I'll trust you, or am I to tell you the whole thing right now?"

"You won't force me to listen to another word from you, if you're a gentleman, Mr. Toye!"

"It's not what I am that counts. Swear that to me, and I swear, on my side, that I won't give him away to you or any one else. But it must be the most solemn contract man and woman ever made."

The silver teapot arrived at this juncture, and not inopportunely. She had to give him his tea, with her young maid's help, and to play a tiny part in which he supported her really beautifully. She had time to think, almost coolly; and one thought brought a thrill. If it was a question of her marrying or not marrying Walter Cazalet, then he must be free, and only the doer of some dreadful deed!

"What *has* he done?" she begged, with a pathetic abandonment of her previous attitude, the moment they were by themselves.

"Must I tell you?" His reluctance rang genuine.

"I insist upon it!" she flashed again.

"Well, it's a long story."

"Never mind. I can listen."

"You know, I had to go back to Italy——"

"Had you?"

"Well, I did go." He had slurred the first statement; this one was characteristically deliberate. "I did go, and before I went I asked Cazalet for an introduction to some friends of his down in Rome."

"I didn't know he had any," said Blanche. She was not listening so very well; she was, in fact, instinctively prepared to challenge every statement, on Cazalet's behalf; and here her instinct defeated itself.

"No more he has," said Toye, "but he claimed to have some. He left the *Kaiser Fritz* the other day at Naples—just when I came aboard. I guess he told you?"

"No. I understood he came round to Southampton. Surely you shared a cabin?"

"Only from Genoa; that's where Cazalet rejoined the steamer."

"Well?"

"He claimed to have spent the interval mostly with friends in Rome. Those friends don't exist, Miss Blanche," said Toye.

"Is that any business of mine?" she asked him squarely.

"Why, yes, I'm afraid it's going to be. That is, unless you'll still trust me—"

"Go on, please."

"Why, he never stayed in Rome at all, nor yet in Italy any longer than it takes to come through on the train. Your attention for one moment!" He took out a neat pocketbook. Blanche had opened her lips, but she did not interrupt; she just grasped the arms of her chair, as though about to bear physical pain. "The *Kaiser Fritz*"—Toye was speaking from his book—"got to Naples late Monday afternoon, September eighth. She was overdue, and I was mad about it, and madder still when I went aboard and she never sailed till morning. I guess I'd wasted—"

"Do tell me about Walter Cazalet!" cried Blanche. It was like small talk from a dentist at the last moment.

"I want you to understand about the steamer first," said Toye. "She waited Monday night in the Bay of Naples, only sailed Tuesday morning, only reached Genoa Wednesday morning, and lay there forty-eight hours, as the German boats do, anyhow. That brings us to Friday morning before the *Kaiser Fritz* gets quit of Italy, doesn't it?"

"Yes—do tell me about Walter!"

"He was gone ashore Monday evening before I came aboard at Naples. I never saw him till he scrambled aboard again Friday, about the fifty-ninth minute of the eleventh hour."

"At Genoa?"

"Sure."

"And you pretend to know where he'd been?"

"I guess I do know"—and Toye sighed as he raised his little book. "Cazalet stepped on the train that left Naples six fifty Monday evening, and off the one timed to reach Charing Cross three twenty-five Wednesday."

"The day of the m—"

"Yes. I never called it by the hardest name, myself; but it was seven thirty Wednesday evening that Henry Craven got his death-blow somehow. Well, Walter Cazalet left Charing Cross again by the nine o'clock that night, and was back aboard the *Kaiser Fritz* on Friday morning—full of his friends in Rome who didn't exist!"

The note-book was put away with every symptom of relief.

"I suppose you can prove what you say?" said Blanche in a voice as dull as her unseeing eyes.

"I have men to swear to him—ticket-collectors, conductors, waiters on the restaurant-car—all up and down the line. I went over the same ground on the same trains, so that was simple. I can also produce the barber who claims to have taken off his beard in Paris, where he put in hours Thursday morning."

Blanche looked up suddenly, not at Toye, but past him toward an overladen side-table against the wall. It was there that Cazalet's photograph had stood among many others; until this morning she had never missed it, for she seemed hardly to have been in her room all the week; but she had been wondering who had removed it, whether Cazalet himself (who had spoken of doing so, she now knew why), or Martha (whom she would not question about it) in a fit of ungovernable disapproval. And now there was the photograph back in its place, leather frame and all!

"I know what you did," said Blanche. "You took that photograph with you— the one on that table—and had him identified by it!"

Yet she stated the fact, for his bowed head admitted it to be one, as nothing but a fact, in the same dull voice of apathetic acquiescence in an act of which the man himself was ashamed. She could see him wondering at her; she even wondered at herself. Yet if all this were true, what matter how the truth had come to light?

"It was the night I came down to bid you good-by," he confessed, "and didn't have time to wait. I didn't come down for the photo. I never thought of it till I saw it there. I came down to kind of warn you, Miss Blanche!"

"Against him?" she said, as if there was only one man left in the world.

"Yes—I guess I'd already warned Cazalet that I was starting on his tracks."

And then Blanche just said, "Poor—old—Sweep!" as one talking to herself. And Toye seized upon the words as she had seized on nothing from him.

"Have you only pity for the fellow?" he cried; for she was gazing at the bearded photograph without revulsion.

"Of course," she answered, hardly attending.

"Even though he killed this man—even though he came across Europe to kill him?"

"You don't think it was deliberate yourself, even if he did do it."

"But can you doubt that he did?" cried Toye, quick to ignore the point she had made, yet none the less sincerely convinced upon the other. "I guess you wouldn't if you'd heard some of the things he said to me on the steamer; and he's made good every syllable since he landed. Why, it explains every single thing he's done and left undone. He'll strain every nerve to have Scruton ably defended, but he won't see the man he's defending; says himself that he can't face him!"

"Yes. He said so to me," said Blanche, nodding in confirmation.

"To you?"

"I didn't understand him."

"But you're been seeing him all this while?"

"Every day," said Blanche, her soft eyes filling suddenly. "We've had—we've had the time of our lives!"

"My God!" said Toye. "The time of your life with a man who's got another man's blood on his hands—and that makes no difference to you! The time of your life with the man who knew where to lay hands on the weapon he'd done it with, who went as far as that to save the innocent, but no farther!"

"He would; he will still, if it's still necessary. You don't know him, Mr. Toye; you haven't known him all your life."

"And all this makes no difference to a good and gentle woman—one of the gentlest and the best God ever made?"

"If you mean me, I won't go so far as that," said Blanche. "I must see him first."

"See Cazalet?"

Toye had come to his feet, not simply in the horror and indignation which had gradually taken possession of him, but under the stress of some new and sudden resolve.

"Of course," said Blanche; "of course I must see him as soon as possible."

"Never again!" he cried.

"What?"

"You shall never speak to that man again, as long as ever you live," said Toye, with the utmost emphasis and deliberation.

"Who's going to prevent me?"

"I am."

"How?"

"By laying an information against him this minute, unless you promise never to see or to speak to Cazalet again."

Blanche felt cold and sick, but the bit of downright bullying did her good. "I didn't know you were a blackmailer, Mr. Toye!"

"You know I'm not; but I mean to save you from Cazalet, blackmail or white."

"To save me from a mere old friend—nothing more—*nothing*—all our lives!"

"I believe that," he said, searching her with his smoldering eyes. "You couldn't tell a lie, I guess, not if you tried! But you would do something; it's just a man being next door to hell that would bring a God's angel—" His voice shook.

She was as quick to soften on her side.

"Don't talk nonsense, please," she begged, forcing a smile through her distress. "Will you promise to do nothing if—if *I* promise?"

"Not to go near him?"

"No."

"Nor to see him here?"

"No."

"Nor anywhere else?"

"No. I give you my word."

"If you break it, I break mine that minute? Is it a deal that way?"

"Yes! Yes! I promise!"

"Then so do I, by God!" said Hilton Toye.

# XIV
# FAITH UNFAITHFUL

"It's all perfectly true," said Cazalet calmly. "Those were my movements while I was off the ship, except for the five hours and a bit that I was away from Charing Cross. I can't dispute a detail of all the rest. But they'll have to fill in those five hours unless they want another case to collapse like the one against Scruton!"

Old Savage had wriggled like a venerable worm, in the experienced talons of the Bobby's Bugbear; but then Mr. Drinkwater and his discoveries had come still worse out of a hotter encounter with the truculent attorney; and Cazalet had described the whole thing as only he could describe a given episode, down to the ultimate dismissal of the charge against Scruton, with a gusto the more cynical for the deliberately low pitch of his voice. It was in the little lodging-house sitting-room at Nell Gwynne's Cottages; he stood with his back to the crackling fire that he had just lighted himself, as it were, already at bay; for the folding-doors were in front of his nose, and his eyes roved incessantly from the landing door on one side to the curtained casement on the other. Yet sometimes he paused to gaze at the friend who had come to warn him of his danger; and there was nothing cynical or grim about him then.

Blanche had broken her word for perhaps the first time in her life; but it had never before been extorted from her by duress, and it would be affectation to credit her with much compunction on the point. Her one great qualm lay in the possibility of Toye's turning up at any moment; but this she had obviated to some extent by coming straight to the cottages when he left her—presumably to look for Cazalet in London, since she had been careful not to mention his change of address. Cazalet, to her relief, but also a little to her hurt, she had found at his lodgings in the neighborhood, full of the news he had not managed to communicate to her. But it was no time for taking anything but his peril to heart. And that they had been discussing, almost as man to man, if rather as innocent man to innocent man; for even now, or perhaps now in his presence least of all, Blanche could not bring herself to believe her old friend guilty of a violent crime, however unpremeditated, for which another had been allowed to suffer, for however short a time.

And yet, he seemed to make no secret of it; and yet—it did explain his whole conduct since landing, as Toye had said.

She could only shut her eyes to what must have happened, even as Cazalet himself had shut his all this wonderful week, that she had forgotten all day in her ingratitude, but would never, in all her days, forget again!

"There won't be another case," she heard herself saying, while her thoughts ran ahead or lagged behind like sheep. "It'll never come out—I know it won't."

"Why shouldn't it?" he asked so sharply that she had to account for the words, to herself as well as to him.

"Nobody knows except Mr. Toye, and he means to keep it to himself."

"Why should he?"

"I don't know. He'll tell you himself."

"Are you sure you don't know? What can he have to tell me? Why should he screen me, Blanche?"

His eyes and voice were furious with suspicion, but still the voice was lowered.

"He's a jolly good sort, you know," said Blanche, as if the whole affair was the most ordinary one in the world. But heroics could not have driven the sense of her remark more forcibly home to Cazalet.

"Oh, he is, is he?"

"I've always found him so."

"So have I, the little I've seen of him. And I don't blame him for getting on my tracks, mind you; he's a bit of a detective, I was fair game, and he did warn me in a way. That's why I meant to have the week—" He stopped and looked away.

"I know. And nothing can undo *that*," she only said; but her voice swelled with thanksgiving. And Cazalet looked reassured; the hot suspicion died out of his eyes, but left them gloomily perplexed.

"Still, I can't understand it. I don't believe it, either! I'm in his hands. What have I done to be saved by Toye? He's probably scouring London for me—if he isn't watching this window at this minute!"

He went to the curtains as he spoke. Simultaneously Blanche sprang up, to entreat him to fly while he could. That had been her first object in coming to him as she had done, and yet, once with him, she had left it to the last! And now it was too late; he was at the window, chuckling significantly to himself; he had opened it, and he was leaning out.

"That you, Toye, down there? Come up and show yourself! I want to see you."

He turned in time to dart in front of the folding-doors as Blanche reached them, white and shuddering. The flush of impulsive bravado fled from his face at the sight of hers.

"You can't go in there. What's the matter?" he whispered. "Why should *you* be afraid of Hilton Toye?"

How could she tell him? Before she had found a word, the landing door opened, and Hilton Toye was in the room, looking at her.

"Keep your voice down," said Cazalet anxiously. "Even if it's all over with me but the shouting, we needn't start the shouting here!"

He chuckled savagely at his jest; and now Toye stood looking at him.

"I've heard all you've done," continued Cazalet. "I don't blame you a bit. If it had been the other way about, I might have given you less run for your money. I've heard what you've found out about my mysterious movements, and you're absolutely right as far as you go. You don't know why I took the train at Naples, and traveled across Europe without a hand-bag. It wasn't quite the put-up job you may think. But, if it makes you any happier, I may as well tell you that I *was* at Uplands that night, and I *did* get out through the foundations!"

The insane impetuosity of the man was his master now. He was a living fire of impulse that had burst into a blaze. His voice was raised in spite of his warning to the others, and the very first sound of Toye's was to remind him that he was forgetting his own advice. Toye had not looked a second time at Blanche; nor did he now; but he took in the silenced Cazalet from head to heel, by inches.

"I always guessed you might be crazy, and I now know it," said Hilton Toye. "Still, I judge you're not so crazy as to deny that while you were in that house you struck down Henry Craven, and left him for dead?"

Cazalet stood like a red-hot stone.

"Miss Blanche," said Toye, turning to her rather shyly, "I guess I can't do what I said just yet. I haven't breathed a word, not yet, and perhaps I never will, if you'll come away with me now—back to your home—and never see Henry Craven's murderer again!"

"And who may he be?" cried a voice that brought all three face-about.

The folding-doors had opened, and a fourth figure was standing between the two rooms.

75

# XV
# THE PERSON UNKNOWN

The intruder was a shaggy elderly man, of so cadaverous an aspect that his face alone cried for his death-bed; and his gaunt frame took up the cry, as it swayed upon the threshold in dressing-gown and bedroom slippers that Toye instantly recognized as belonging to Cazalet. The man had a shock of almost white hair, and a less gray beard clipped roughly to a point. An unwholesome pallor marked the fallen features; and the envenomed eyes burned low in their sockets, as they dealt with Blanche but fastened on Hilton Toye.

"What do *you* know about Henry Craven's murderer?" he demanded in a voice between a croak and a crow. "Have they run in some other poor devil, or were you talking about me? If so, I'll start a libel action, and call Cazalet and that lady as witnesses!"

**"What do you know about Henry Craven's murderer?"**

"This is Scruton," explained Cazalet, "who was only liberated this evening after being detained a week on a charge that ought never to have been brought, as I've told you both all along." Scruton thanked him with a bitter laugh. "I've brought him here," concluded Cazalet, "because I don't think he's fit enough to be about alone."

"Nice of him, isn't it?" said Scruton bitterly. "I'm so fit that they wanted to keep me somewhere else longer than they'd any right; that may be why they lost no time in getting hold of me again. Nice, considerate, kindly country! Ten years isn't long enough to have you as a dishonored guest. 'Won't you come back for another week, and see if we can't arrange a nice little sudden death and burial for you?' But they couldn't you see, blast 'em!"

He subsided into the best chair in the room, which Blanche had wheeled up behind him; a moment later he looked round, thanked her curtly, and lay back with closed eyes until suddenly he opened them on Cazalet.

"And what was that *you* were saying—that about traveling across Europe and being at Uplands that night? I thought you came round by sea? And what night do you mean?"

"The night it all happened," said Cazalet steadily.

"You mean the night some person unknown knocked Craven on the head?"

"Yes."

The sick man threw himself forward in the chair. "You never told me this!" he cried suspiciously; both the voice and the man seemed stronger.

"There was no point in telling you."

"Did you see the person?"

"Yes."

"Then he isn't unknown to you?"

"I didn't see him well."

Scruton looked sharply at the two mute listeners. They were very intent, indeed. "Who are these people, Cazalet? No! I know one of 'em," he answered himself in the next breath. "It's Blanche Macnair, isn't it? I thought at first it must be a younger sister grown up like her. You'll forgive prison manners, Miss Macnair, if that's still your name. You look a woman to trust— if there is one—and you gave me your chair. Anyhow, you've been in for a penny and you can stay in for a pound, as far as I care! But who's your Amer'can friend, Cazalet?"

"Mr. Hilton Toye, who spotted that I'd been all the way to Uplands and back when I claimed to have been in Rome!"

There was a touch of Scruton's bitterness in Cazalet's voice; and by some subtle process it had a distinctly mollifying effect on the really embittered man.

"What on earth were you doing at Uplands?" he asked, in a kind of confidential bewilderment.

"I went down to see a man."

Toye himself could not have cut and measured more deliberate monosyllables.

"Craven?" suggested Scruton.

"No; a man I expected to find at Craven's."

"The writer of the letter you found at Cook's office in Naples the night you landed there, I guess!"

It really was Toye this time, and there was no guesswork in his tone. Obviously he was speaking by his little book, though he had not got it out again.

"How do you know I went to Cook's?"

"I know every step you took between the *Kaiser Fritz* and Charing Cross and Charing Cross and the *Kaiser Fritz*!"

Scruton listened to this interchange with keen attention, hanging on each man's lips with his sunken eyes; both took it calmly, but Scruton's surprise was not hidden by a sardonic grin.

"You've evidently had a stern chase with a Yankee clipper!" said he. "If he's right about the letter, Cazalet, I should say so; presumably it wasn't from Craven himself?"

"No."

"Yet it brought you across Europe to Craven's house?"

"Well—to the back of his house! I expected to meet my man on the river."

"Was that how you missed him more or less?"

"I suppose it was."

Scruton ruminated a little, broke into his offensive laugh, and checked it instantly of his own accord. "This is really interesting," he croaked. "You get to London—at what time was it?"

"Nominally three twenty-five; but the train ran thirteen minutes late," said Hilton Toye.

"And you're on the river by what time?" Scruton asked Cazalet.

"I walked over Hungerford Bridge, took the first train to Surbiton, got a boat there, and just dropped down with the stream. I don't suppose the whole thing took me very much more than an hour."

"Aren't you forgetting something?" said Toye.

"Yes, I was. It was I who telephoned to the house and found that Craven was out motoring; so there was no hurry."

"Yet you weren't going to see Henry Craven?" murmured Toye.

Cazalet did not answer. His last words had come in a characteristic burst; now he had his mouth shut tight, and his eyes were fast to Scruton. He might have been in the witness-box already, a doomed wretch cynically supposed to be giving evidence on his own behalf, but actually only baring his neck by inches to the rope, under the joint persuasion of judge and counsel. But he had one friend by him still, one who had edged a little nearer in the pause.

"But you did see the man you went to see?" said Scruton.

Cazalet paused. "I don't know. Eventually somebody brushed past me in the dark. I did think then—but I can't swear to him even now!"

"Tell us about it."

"Do you mean that, Scruton? Do you insist on hearing all that happened? I'm not asking Toye; he can do what he likes. But you, Scruton—you've been through a lot, you know—you ought to have stopped in bed—do you really want this on top of all?"

"Go ahead," said Scruton. "I'll have a drink when you've done; somebody give me a cigarette meanwhile."

Cazalet supplied the cigarette, struck the match, and held it with unfaltering hand. The two men's eyes met strangely across the flame.

"I'll tell you all exactly what happened; you can believe me or not as you like. You won't forget that I knew every inch of the ground—except one altered bit that explained itself." Cazalet turned to Blanche with a significant look, but she only drew an inch nearer still. "Well, it was in the little creek, where the boat-house is, that I waited for my man. He never came—by the river. I heard the motor, but it wasn't Henry Craven that I wanted to see, but the man who was coming to see him. Eventually I thought I must have made a mistake, or he might have changed his mind and come by road. The dressing-gong had gone; at least I supposed it was that by the time. It was almost quite dark, and I landed and went up the path past the back premises to the front of the house. So far I hadn't seen a soul, or been seen by one, evidently; but the French windows were open in what used to be my father's library, the room was all lit up, and just as I got there a man ran out into the flood of light and—"

"I thought you said he brushed by you in the dark?" interrupted Toye.

"I was in the dark; so was he in another second; and no power on earth would induce me to swear to him. Do you want to hear the rest, Scruton, or are you another unbeliever?"

"I want to hear every word—more than ever!"

Toye cocked his head at both question and answer, but inclined it quickly as Cazalet turned to him before proceeding.

"I went in and found Henry Craven lying in his blood. That's gospel—it was so I found him—lying just where he had fallen in a heap out of the leather chair at his desk. The top right-hand drawer of his desk was open, the key in it and the rest of the bunch still swinging! A revolver lay as it had dropped upon the desk—it had upset the ink—and there were cartridges lying loose in the open drawer, and the revolver was loaded. I swept it back into the drawer, turned the key and removed it with the bunch. But there was something else on the desk—that silver-mounted truncheon—and a man's cap was lying on the floor. I picked them both up. My first instinct, I confess it, was to remove every sign of manslaughter and to leave the scene to be reconstructed into one of accident—seizure—anything but what it was!"

He paused as if waiting for a question. None was asked. Toye's mouth might have been sewn up, his eyes were like hatpins driven into his head. The other two simply stared.

"It was a mad idea, but I had gone mad," continued Cazalet. "I had hated the victim alive, and it couldn't change me that he was dead or dying; *that* didn't make him a white man, and neither did it necessarily blacken the poor devil who had probably suffered from him like the rest of us and only struck him down in self-defense. The revolver on the desk made that pretty plain. It was out of the way, but now I saw blood all over the desk as well; it was soaking into the blotter, and it knocked the bottom out of my idea. What was to be done? I had meddled already; how could I give the alarm without giving myself away to that extent, and God knows how much further? The most awful moment of the lot came as I hesitated—the dinner-gong went off in the hall outside the door! I remember watching the thing on the floor to see if it would move.

"Then I lost my head—absolutely. I turned the key in the door, to give myself a few seconds' grace or start; it reminded me of the keys in my hands. One of them was one of those little round bramah keys. It seemed familiar to me even after so many years. I looked up, and there was my father's Michelangelo closet, with its little round bramah keyhole. I opened it as the outer door was knocked at and then tried. But my mad instinct of altering every possible appearance, to mislead the police, stuck to me to the last. And I took the man's watch and chain into the closet with me, as well as the cap and truncheon that I had picked up before.

"I don't know how long I was above ground, so to speak, but one of my father's objects had been to make his retreat sound-tight, and I could scarcely hear what was going on in the room. That encouraged me; and two of you don't need telling how I got out through the foundations, because you know all about the hole I made myself as a boy in the floor under the oilcloth. It took some finding with single matches; but the fear of your neck gives you eyes in your finger-ends, and gimlets, too, by Jove! The worst part was getting out at the other end, into the cellars; there were heaps of empty bottles to move, one by one, before there was room to open the manhole door and to squirm out over the slab; and I thought they rang like a peal of bells, but I put them all back again, and apparently … nobody overheard in the scullery.

"The big dog barked at me like blazes—he did again the other day—but nobody seemed to hear him either. I got to my boat, tipped a fellow on the towing path to take it back and pay for it—why haven't the police got hold of him?—and ran down to the bridge over the weir. I stopped a big car with a smart shaver smoking his pipe at the wheel. I should have thought he'd have come forward for the reward that was put up; but I pretended I was late for dinner I had in town, and I let him drop me at the Grand Hotel. He cost me a fiver, but I had on a waistcoat lined with notes, and I'd more than five minutes in hand at Charing Cross. If you want to know, it was the time in hand that gave me the whole idea of doubling back to Genoa; I must have been half-way up to town before I thought of it!"

He had told the whole thing as he always could tell an actual experience; that was one reason why it rang so true to one listener at every point. But the sick man's sunken eyes had advanced from their sockets in cumulative amazement. And Hilton Toye laughed shortly when the end was reached.

"You figure some on our credulity!" was his first comment.

"I don't figure on anything from you, Toye, except a pair of handcuffs as a first instalment!"

Toye rose in prompt acceptance of the challenge. "Seriously, Cazalet, you ask us to believe that you did all this to screen a man you didn't have time to recognize?"

"I've told you the facts."

"Well, I guess you'd better tell them to the police." Toye took his hat and stick. Scruton was struggling from his chair. Blanche stood petrified, a dove under a serpent's spell, as Toye made her a sardonic bow from the landing door. "You broke your side of the contract, Miss Blanche! I guess it's up to me to complete."

"Wait!"

It was Scruton's raven croak; he had tottered to his feet.

"Sure," said Toye, "if you've anything you want to say as an interested party."

"Only this—he's told the truth!"

"Well, can he prove it?"

"I don't know," said Scruton. "But I can!"

"You?" Blanche chimed in there.

"Yes, I'd like that drink first, if you don't mind, Cazalet." It was Blanche who got it for him, in an instant. "Thank you! I'd say more if my blessing was worth having—but here's something that is. Listen to this, you American gentleman: I was the man who wrote to him in Naples. Leave it at that a minute; it was my second letter to him; the first was to Australia, in answer to one from him. It was the full history of my downfall. I got a warder to smuggle it out. That letter was my one chance."

"I know it by heart," said Cazalet. "It was that and nothing else that made me leave before the shearing."

"To meet me when I came out!" Scruton explained in a hoarse whisper. "To—to keep me from going straight to that man, as I'd told him I should in my first letter! But you can't hit these things off to the day or the week; he'd told me where to write to him on his voyage, and I wrote to Naples, but that letter did not get smuggled out. My warder friend had got the sack. I had to put what I'd got to say so that you could read it two ways. So I told you, Cazalet, I was going straight up the river for a row—and you can pronounce that two ways. And I said I hoped I shouldn't break a scull—but there's another way of spelling that, and it was the other way I meant!" He chuckled grimly. "I wanted you to lie low and let *me* lie low if that happened. I wanted just one man in the world to know I'd done it. But that's how we came to miss each other, for you timed it to a tick, if you hadn't misread me about the river."

He drank again, stood straighter, and found a fuller voice.

"Yet I never meant to do it unless he made me, and at the back of my brain I never thought he would. I thought he'd do something for me, after all he'd done before! Shall I tell you what he did?"

"Got out his revolver!" cried Cazalet in a voice that was his own justification as well.

"Pretending it was going to be his check-book!" said Scruton through his teeth. "But I heard him trying to cock it inside his drawer. There was his special constable's truncheon hanging on the wall—silver mounted, for all the world to know how he'd stood up for law and order in the sight of men! I tell you it was a joy to feel the weight of that truncheon, and to see the hero of Trafalgar Square fumbling with a thing he didn't understand! I hit him as hard as God would let me—and the rest you know—except that I nearly did trip over the man who swore it was broad daylight at the time!"

He tottered to the folding-doors, and stood there a moment, pointing to Cazalet with a hand that twitched as terribly as his dreadful face.

"No—the rest you did—the rest you did to save what wasn't worth saving! But—I think—I'll hold out long enough to thank you—just a little!" He was gone with a gibbering smile.

Cazalet turned straight to Toye at the other door. "Well? Aren't you going, too? You were near enough, you see! I'm an accessory all right"—he dropped his voice—"but I'd be principal if I could instead of *him!*"

But Toye had come back into the room, twinkling with triumph, even rubbing his hands. "You didn't see? You didn't see? I never meant to go at all; it was a bit of bluff to make him own up, and it did, too, bully!"

The couple gasped.

"You mean to tell me," cried Cazalet, "that you believed my story all the time?"

"Why, I didn't have a moment's doubt about it!"

Cazalet drew away from the chuckling creature and his crafty glee. But Blanche came forward and held out her hand.

"Will you forgive me, Mr. Toye?"

"Sure, if I had anything to forgive. It's the other way around, I guess, and about time I did something to help." He edged up to the folding-door. "This is a two-man job, Cazalet, the way I make it out. Guess it's my watch on deck!"

"The other's the way to the police station," said Cazalet densely.

Toye turned solemn on the word. "It's the way to hell, if Miss Blanche will forgive me! This is more like the other place, thanks to you folks. Guess I'll leave the angels in charge!"

Angelic or not, the pair were alone at last; and through the doors they heard a quavering croak of welcome to the rather human god from the American machine.

"I'm afraid he'll never go back with you to the bush," whispered Blanche.

"Scruton?"

"Yes."

"I'm afraid, too. But I wanted to take somebody else out, too. I was trying to say so over a week ago, when we were talking about old Venus Potts. Blanchie, will you come?"

## THE END